TREE

OF

DREAMS

TREE

OF

DREAMS

Ten Tales from the Garden of Night

BY LAURENCE YEP

PICTURES BY ISADORE SELTZER

BridgeWater Books

To my fellow dreamer, Joanne.
L.Y.

To Joyce, who makes me think.
To Larry, who makes me laugh.
To my mother, who made me draw.
To my father, who made me work.
I.S.

Text copyright © 1995 by Laurence Yep.
Illustrations copyright © 1995 by Isadore Seltzer.
Published by BridgeWater Books, an imprint of Troll Associates, Inc.
Printed in the United States of America.
10 9 8 7 6 5 4 3 2 1

Yep, Laurence.
Tree of dreams: ten tales from the garden of night / by Laurence Yep;
illustrated by Isadore Seltzer.
p.   cm.
Includes bibliographical references.
Contents: The helpful badger — Dream girl — Fighting cricket — South branch —
The rescue — Paying with shadows — The dream tree — The loom of night —
The buried treasure — The fool's dream.
ISBN 0-8167-3498-4
1. Dreams — Folklore.   2. Tales.   [1. Dreams — Folklore.   2. Folklore.]
I. Seltzer, Isadore, ill.   II. Title.
PZ8.1.Y37Tr   1995   [398.2] — dc20   [398.27]   94-11250

CONTENTS

PREFACE

There is a tree of dreams. Its roots reach deep into the dark, fertile soil of night. From these roots rise our visions, weaving together until they are as thick and dense as the trunk of a tree.

What happens at night when we sleep? While our bodies lie still, we can see and taste and touch things that seem so real. Sometimes they seem more real than when we are awake.

Dreaming is a bond that unites us—beyond language and custom, beyond geography and time itself. For every night, we all return to the tree of dreams—from a child in the Amazon jungle to one in a Chinese city, from a weaver in Africa to a slave in India. We are all entwined among the multitude of branches as our first ancestors were, for dreaming reaches across time to the very beginning of humanity. In fact, the indigenous peoples of Australia refer to the time of creation as the Dreamtime.

Every culture has attempted to explain the dream experience in story; in turn, these stories have branched off in many directions. One of the earliest recorded dreams is of King Gudea from the city of Lagash in the land of Sumeria in about 2250 B.C. In it, his god, Nin-Girsu, instructs him on how to build a temple, a prophecy King Gudea later fulfills.

Here are ten stories about those who have ascended the tree of dreams. Each tale is a different branch, giving us a new perspective on dreams and dreaming. Beside a stove in Alexandria, we learn about the fleeting nature of dreams. From the floor of an Indian palace, we see what we can achieve.

From such perches, we may catch a glimpse not only of a different patch of the universe but of one another, as well.

ANIMAL GUARDIANS

In many societies around the world—including certain Native American cultures—people seek animal spirits to guide and protect them. In this Japanese tale, an animal spirit repays the favor of a kindly man. The dream provides the medium by which the animal, unable to communicate in the real world, can speak to his friend.

The Helpful Badger

(Japan)

Once in Japan, there was a man named Kitabayashi. On the day that his son got married, he invited family, friends, and neighbors to a feast. There were all sorts of good things to eat, but the man made sure everyone ate some *sekihan*—a special dish of rice and red beans that was thought to bring good luck.

The guests were having such a good time that the party went on late into the night. Although there had been many people, there was still a great deal of food left over.

When the last guest had gone, Mr. Kitabayashi yawned. "It is late," he said to his wife. "Let's put everything away in the morning."

Relieved, the couple left everything where it was and went to bed. Around midnight, Mr. Kitabayashi was awakened by a noise. As he lay on his mat, he heard another thump from the next room.

Quietly, he got up and crept out into the hallway. From within the room, he heard thumps and bumps. Is it thieves? he asked himself, suddenly afraid. Slowly, he slid back a screen door and peeked inside the room.

Roaming over the floor mats were twelve creatures. Some were young; others were gray-backed elders. They waddled about on their short, stubby legs, sniffing at this or that. "Badgers! I wonder how they got in," he muttered to himself, then went to get a broom to chase them out.

When he returned, he found them all gathered around a bowl of *sekihan*. The younger ones tried to thrust their muzzles in, but the older ones rapped them sharply. Then, while the younger ones watched, the elders dipped their paws in and scooped out handfuls of *sekihan*, careful not to drop any on the floor. Mr. Kitabayashi chuckled to himself. "It's almost as if the parents are teaching the young ones manners."

Tickled, he watched the badgers eat hungrily. He noticed how thin they all looked. "Times must be hard, eh?" he whispered. "Poor badgers. Are you having trouble finding enough to eat? You must be, or why would you sneak in here?" He thought for a moment and then smiled. "I've known what it's like to be hungry. I will share our good fortune with you, for this has been a happy day."

Sliding the door shut, the kindly man put away the broom and went back to bed. "What was that noise?" his wife asked.

"Just a few guests," Mr. Kitabayashi said. "They arrived late."

"They've got some nerve," the wife said. "Did you tell them to go home?"

Mr. Kitabayashi thought of the badger family. "They'll leave soon. They've kept on their coats."

"How rude," his wife complained.

"They're not so bad," he replied. "Let's not spoil their fun." He rolled over.

However, his wife nudged him. "Well, who are they?"

"Mr. and Mrs. Badger," he mumbled sleepily.

"Badgers! In my house! They'll make a mess of everything," Mrs. Kitabayashi said, poking him urgently. "Go chase them away."

But after twenty years of marriage, Mr. Kitabayashi's back was like iron to his wife's elbow. "Not these badgers. They're very well behaved." Mr. Kitabayashi went back to sleep.

"If you aren't the oddest man," his wife said with a sigh, but she was so tired from the day that she fell asleep, too.

The next morning, the mess was exactly as they had left it — though the *sekihan* bowl had been licked completely clean. "You see," Mr. Kitabayashi said cheerfully, "I told you the badgers were polite guests."

After they had cleaned up the house, Mr. Kitabayashi went looking for a hole in the wall. When he found it, he covered it up carefully. But all the rest of the day, he felt guilty. "I wonder if the little ones are getting enough to eat?" So that evening after supper, he put out some of the leftovers outside their house.

His wife watched him, mystified. "Aren't you the strangest man? Why are you doing that?"

"It's for last night's guests," Mr. Kitabayashi said, and he told her about what he had seen.

His wife was not sure that it was such a good idea. "You'll just encourage them to come back. Badgers can be pretty rowdy animals."

"Not these badgers," Mr. Kitabayashi insisted. "They have good manners."

Since her husband was set on putting out food, Mrs. Kitabayashi stopped arguing.

The next day, all the food was gone. Mr. Kitabayashi held up the empty bowl. "You see, they did come."

"Humph, we're probably just feeding some stray cat," his wife mumbled. But that night, she let him set out more leftovers. She would have gone to bed, but Mr. Kitabayashi wanted her to stay up and see whether they came again.

"You're getting odder and odder," Mrs. Kitabayashi said in exasperation.

Her husband held onto her hand. "Perhaps, but sit with me awhile. There will be a full moon tonight. Remember how we used to sit and watch it?"

"For old time's sake, then." She pretended to grumble, but she wanted to keep an eye out inside their house.

Sure enough, as the moon rose, they watched the badgers trot toward the house with their peculiar gait. Their powerful, broad backs seemed to roll up and down. In the moonlight, their fur shone all silvery.

When the badgers encircled the bowl, they began to dip their paws in politely. "You see, it is just like I said." Mr. Kitabayashi nudged his wife.

"They're so cute," she replied.

From then on, they left food out every night. Sometimes, Mrs. Kitabayashi even made special treats for the badger family.

Then one night, Mr. Kitabayashi heard a thump inside his house. Believing that the badgers had returned, he blinked sleepily. That's gratitude for you, he thought. They've broken into our house again.

As he started to get up to scold them, the bedroom door slid to the side. Two tall shadowy figures stood in the doorway. These were no badgers.

"W-w-who are you?" stammered Mr. Kitabayashi.

Shutting the door behind them, they padded noiselessly into the room. In the moonlight, Mr. Kitabayashi saw two men. A sword blade flashed as one man drew it out. "Tell us where you have your money," the swordsman demanded.

Mr. Kitabayashi hid under the comforter and clung to his wife. "I-I-I have no money in the house."

The thief held the sword next to his throat. "Don't lie, or we'll kill you."

Suddenly, there was a loud noise in the house. The thieves straightened and turned. "What's that?" one of them asked just as the bedroom door crashed down.

Two huge wrestlers stood in the doorway. They looked as solid as boulders with legs. One wrestler pointed toward the street for the thieves to go. Then he lifted his large hands and flexed the fingers menacingly—the robbers would face those hands if they stayed.

"You can't scare me while I have this." The swordsman raised his blade above his head and brought it down in a wicked slash. But as large as the wrestler was, he was also lightning-quick. Leaping nimbly to the side, he caught the swordsman's wrist.

With a flip and a twist, he turned the swordsman head over heels until the thief was flat on his back. Then the wrestler adjusted his grip and tightened it until the swordsman cried out in pain. When the sword clattered to the floor, the wrestler kicked it over to his partner, who picked it up.

Turning, the first wrestler glowered at the other thief. Again he pointed toward the street. Then he stamped his foot so hard that the house seemed to shake.

"Yes, whatever you say," the second thief babbled, and he helped his moaning companion to his feet. Then they dashed out of the house and were never seen again.

"You have our eternal gratitude," Mr. Kitabayashi said. He and his wife got to their knees and bowed thankfully until their foreheads touched the floor. When they straightened up, the wrestlers had vanished.

"How could anyone so big be so quiet?" Mrs. Kitabayashi asked. They looked all around the house and then out at the street, but there was no sign of their rescuers.

"Who could it be?" Mr. Kitabayashi asked his wife.

"It must have been someone magical," his wife said. "But who?"

Although they sat up for a while, trying to figure out who had rescued them, it was still a mystery. Finally, when they were both so exhausted they could not keep their eyes open, they went to sleep.

Mr. Kitabayashi dreamed that he and his wife were sitting in their guest room in their best clothes. Then the screen door slid back and in waddled one badger after another, until they had formed a row in front of them.

At last, the largest and oldest badger stepped forward and bowed its head. "We cannot express our gratitude when you are awake. So we come in this dream to thank you. Food has been scarce of late. Without your generosity, we would have starved."

Mr. Kitabayashi was embarrassed for thinking of such intelligent creatures as pets. "Think nothing of it."

The badger raised a paw. "We would be beasts if we weren't grateful. That is why we came to your rescue."

"So it was *you* who saved us," Mr. Kitabayashi cried in delight.

"We can take many forms," the badger told him. "From now on, rest easy at night, for one of us will always be guarding you."

"And you will never go hungry," Mr. Kitabayashi promised.

"Now, in your honor, my daughters will dance," the badger said, and he sat up on his haunches. As he took a breath, his belly suddenly swelled up, and softly he began to beat time on his stomach. *"Teketen-teketen-teketen."* Then the mother joined in. *"Dokodon-dokodon-dokodon."*

One of the young ones rose on her hind legs. "We wish your family well," she said sweetly, and she did a little dance like one of the wedding guests had done. She set her hind paws down with delicate pats on the floor mats, her claws clicking in time to the drumbeat. *"Pom-poko pom,"* she began to sing. *"Pom-poko pom."*

Another youngster leapt up and joined in. The Kitabayashis watched, fascinated, until the dance had stopped. Then with another bow, the badgers waddled out.

The next morning, Mr. Kitabayashi could not wait to tell his wife. "I just had the oddest dream." And he told her about the badgers' visit.

"Your oddness must be catching," his wife said, "because I dreamed the same thing."

That night, and every night after that, the Kitabayashis left food for the badgers. Sometimes they saw a peculiar, large rock by their front door that had not been there during the day and was gone the next morning. Then they would leave a cup of tea, for they knew it was a badger bodyguard.

DREAMS AND LOVE

Dreams and love go hand in hand. We would all like to believe that there is a special someone for us. In this ancient Indian tale, a dream provides the path to our heart's desire. Almost every other culture has a similar story.

Dream Girl

(India)

There once was a King Chandra, who had a son named Rama. When Rama grew up, the king told his son, "It's time you married and had children."

Though Rama had his doubts, he had to obey his father. So the king sent out his servants to find a suitable princess for his son. Rama went to sleep one evening with marriage very much on his mind.

That night, he dreamed he was walking through a grove of tall coconut trees. Palm leaves waved silently over his head. Beyond was a ring of sweet-fruited guava trees. Then there was a circle of betel-nut trees. Within that third circle was a row of copal trees that grew like a wall surrounding a garden. Every sort of rare flower grew within the garden. The scents were so thick that they made the air as heady as wine. A river ran through the very center of the garden; within the middle of the river stood an island.

On the island was a palace of glass. Walls and towers, gates and floors, all were transparent. Rama could see through room after room. Within the very heart of the palace sat a beautiful woman with skin of gold and hair dark and floating as a cloud. She wore a glittering robe covered with rubies, emeralds, and diamonds. More sparkling jewels decorated her black hair like stars. But her smile was the most dazzling of all.

The prince instantly fell in love with her. The very sight of her made him feel drunk. "Who are you?" he called to her.

"I am Amba," she answered from within the palace. "Who are you?"

Rama told her his name. Eager to meet her, he looked for a bridge, but there was none. Finally, he tried to swim across. As soon as he entered the water, he woke up.

The amazed Rama lay in bed for a long time. The princess in his dream had seemed so vivid. He knew her smile, her eyes, and every strand of her hair. "There is no one else in the world for me," he said.

When the prince told his father, the king said, "She is only a fantasy."

"I have had a vision of my true love. I can marry no other," the prince swore.

His father was still afraid there was no such girl or palace, but he sent out more servants to search for them.

At the same time, in a distant land, a princess by the name of Amba woke from the most wondrous sleep. Eagerly, she told her maid, Urvashi, that she had met a young man named Rama in her dreams.

Urvashi was a wise woman and a good friend to her mistress. She tried to convince Princess Amba that she had just imagined Rama.

"I can never be happy without him," the princess insisted, then went to tell her father.

Amba's father also tried to convince her that Rama was not real. "Just forget this dream boy. If you're going to marry anyone, you can marry that nice Prince Ruplal."

However, the princess refused to consider anyone else. The more stubborn she was, the angrier her father became, until he ordered her imprisoned in the crystal palace. "When you change your mind about Prince Ruplal," her father told her, "you can come out."

So the princess was rowed across the river to the island where the crystal palace was. Urvashi went with her to see to her needs, but everyone else was forbidden to go near the river.

As the princess wept within her transparent prison, Prince Rama suffered, as well. He could not eat or sleep. When his father saw how pale and sad his prince was, he begged Rama to forget his dream. "If you keep on like this, I fear you will die," the concerned king said.

"If she is not real, then I do not want to live," the prince said.

Now, it happened that Prince Rama had a good friend named Luxman. When he heard about the dream, he went to visit the prince. He was upset when he saw how ill the prince appeared.

"I think I know this place," Luxman said. "My mother often spoke of her homeland before she died. In that land is a crystal palace surrounded by a river and gardens and rings of trees."

The prince sat up excitedly. "That was all in my dream."

"But I do not know if the king has a daughter named Amba or what she is like," Luxman warned.

As soon as he heard that part of his dream might be real, the prince had only one desire. He embraced his friend gratefully. "You have restored my hope. Now I must go to this land and find my dream girl."

"It is very far away," Luxman warned.

"I will have no peace, no sleep, no happiness until I do," the prince said. "But it is not your dream. You can stay here. Just don't tell my father what you have told me."

"I am your friend," Luxman said loyally. "I will go with you. But this is what you need to do: Tell your father that you want to learn more of the world before you marry. Ask him for neither elephants nor servants. They will slow us down. The one thing you must request is his old warhorse."

So Rama, accompanied by his friend, sought out the king and told him that he desired to travel and see the world.

The king shook his head. "What's made you so restless lately? It's time you gave up these foolish notions and got married."

Luxman bowed low. "Your Majesty," he said, "wise people say that travel rounds out any person, from prince to commoner. When you are young and restless like Prince Rama, you fall in love with impossible things—the more impossible, the better. That's why he's come up with this crazy notion of marrying a dream woman. Let him experience a little of the world and he will lose that wildness. And then he will settle down and marry a real woman."

The king saw the wisdom of this and turned to his son. "Very well, you may travel. How many elephants and servants will you need?"

"I want neither," Rama said. "All I ask is your old warhorse."

The king gave his permission, and that very day, Rama and Luxman set out upon the old charger. It was a powerful beast that had carried the king through many battles. Though it was old now, it was as strong as when it had been young.

On the horse, they forded rivers and crossed mountains. No obstacle could keep the prince from finding the woman of his dreams. At last, they reached the former homeland of Luxman's mother. Luxman knew it well from her descriptions. Although some things had changed, much had not, and Luxman had no trouble guiding them straight to the crystal palace.

Luxman would have preferred to go into the city to make inquiries first, but Rama was too impatient. He had to see whether this princess was indeed the woman he had dreamed of. Tying up their horse, Luxman and Rama walked through the different rings of trees and the garden until they came to the river.

The crystal palace on its island in the middle of the river shone in the sun. In Rama's dream, he had seen neither the swift currents nor the hungry crocodiles that waited within the water.

"What shall we do?" the prince asked Luxman.

"I'll think of something," Luxman said. While Luxman studied the river, the prince tried to catch a glimpse of his princess. Finally, Rama thought he saw a glittering speck. "There she is," he said excitedly.

Both Rama and Luxman were so busy, they did not notice the guardsmen protecting the palace until it was too late. "What are you doing here?" the commander shouted as his patrol rode up. "No one may look upon Princess Amba."

Though Rama protested, they were marched straight to a complex of buildings by the river, just outside the garden and the rings of trees. There were warehouses grouped around a square.

Despite the king's law, there were still so many suitors that they had filled the royal prison. For convenience sake, one of the buildings had been converted into a jail, but at that moment, it was empty and unwatched. Once Rama and Luxman were put inside, though, the officer detailed a guard.

As he stared through the bars toward the crystal palace, Rama sighed. "The princess is real, but unless we can get out, we might just as well have stayed at home."

"Don't give up yet." Luxman went to the prison door and called to the guardsman at the gate of the complex, "What terrible thing has the princess done to be locked up?"

The guardsman laughed. "She plans to marry a dream boy."

"Did you hear?" Rama said rapturously.

"Yes," Luxman said, then thought a bit. Finally, he called to the guardsman again. When the soldier came over, Luxman took out a purse of gold he had hidden in his clothes.

The guardsman shook his head. "It is no good trying to bribe me. It would be my head if the king discovered I had let you go."

Luxman jingled the purse through the bars of the door. "You can have all this if you will only shout out that Prince Rama has lost his cow and is looking for it."

The guardsman considered the bribe for a moment. Reciting words of nonsense was clearly not the same as releasing prisoners. So he took the gold and did as Luxman had asked.

Just as Luxman had thought, the princess heard the guardsman shouting out the news.

"So they are guarding the prison," she said. "That must mean there are prisoners. I wonder if it really is Rama, the man from my dream."

The princess was as clever as she was beautiful. Quickly, she worked out a plan. She sent Urvashi to the kitchen to fetch some pastries. When they were packed, Amba pulled a ruby ring from her own finger and gave it to Urvashi, instructing her what to do.

Urvashi got in a boat and rowed to the other shore, for she was allowed to go back and forth on errands for the princess. After picking some flowers from the garden, she hurried to the city gates and asked two beggars to do a favor for the princess. Since Amba had always been kind to them, they readily agreed, so Urvashi had them carry her baskets of flowers and pastries and accompany her to the complex of buildings. When the guard demanded to know her business, she said she was going to the temple.

When they entered the square, Urvashi saw Luxman and Rama within the prison. Going into the temple, she fixed garlands for the statues and then took some pastries over to the guards at the gate. "Silly me, I made too much. Will you help me by eating these?"

The pastries smelled delicious and the guards were only too willing to oblige. As they picnicked at the gate, the maid went back into the square. Beckoning to the beggars, she went over to the improvised prison.

Urvashi drew back the bolt and opened the door. "Quick," she whispered. "The princess sent me. Change clothes with these beggars."

Rama and Luxman were only too happy to obey. Quickly, the maid shut the beggars inside the prison. Then, picking up the now-empty baskets, Rama and Luxman followed the maid out the gate and to her family's house.

"Young lords," she said, "you made a great mistake in not paying your respects to our king first. No one is allowed near the river. The law is very harsh. If Princess Amba had not thought of a way to free you, you might have stayed in that cell for a quite a while."

"Then the princess is real," Rama said excitedly. "Does she ever speak of me?"

"Yes," Urvashi said. "Will you do what the princess tells you to?"

Luxman and Rama agreed.

On the following day, the guards delivered their captives to the king. "O mighty king, here are two young lords who were trying to break your law."

Upon the advice of Princess Amba, the beggars had been careful to huddle and keep their faces hidden as much as possible. Now they straightened up as she had previously instructed them to do.

The king smiled and pointed. "I know these fellows. I've often given them alms at the city gates."

The guards were astounded, for they also recognized the beggars. "Where did you get these fancy clothes?" the commander insisted.

The beggars spoke as they had been coached by Urvashi. "We were outside the city when two young lords came up. They gave the clothes to us because they were going to become monks and had no more need of them."

Laughing, the king rewarded the beggars for his guards' mistake and sent them away. Then he scolded his guardsmen. "Idiots. Don't you know a prince from a beggar? They were looking for a handout, not the princess's hand." He sent the shamefaced guards away.

Shortly after this, Urvashi fetched the horse from where Rama and Luxman had left it and put it in a stable near her family's house. While they hid inside the home, Urvashi bought them new clothes. Then, following Amba's counsel, Rama and Luxman presented themselves to the king. "Your Majesty, once I had a dream in which I saw a vision of loveliness," Rama said. "I have come all this way to see if your daughter is the one I saw. I have heard that she also has dreamed of a young man. Do I fit her description of him?"

The king studied Rama. "It's true there is a resemblance, but it must be a coincidence. You might as well give up this preposterous fantasy, young man. My daughter is going to marry Prince Ruplal."

Urvashi had coached Prince Rama well. "Could a fantasy give me this as a token of her love?" Prince Rama asked. Then he produced the ruby ring that Urvashi had passed on to him from Amba.

The king took the ring and examined it carefully. Then he sat back in amazement. "It is indeed my daughter's ring. But how could you have gotten it?"

Prince Rama bowed elegantly. "It is the power of love, Your Majesty."

The king held up his hands. "Who am I to stand in the way of love? Prince Ruplal will just have to understand."

The king called for horses, but Prince Rama got his horse from the stable where Urvashi had put it. Then, with an escort of guards, the entire court left the palace and paraded through the town toward the crystal palace. And as the townsfolk heard the story, they joined the rear of the procession. It was quite a crowd that made its way through the gardens to the princess's shining prison.

When they came to the banks of the river, the king refused to use Urvashi's little rowboat, for it was far too humble for him. Instead, he called for the royal barge.

When Rama saw the crystal palace before him, he grew impatient. Unable to wait for the royal barge, he put the spurs to his horse. The great horse leapt into the air as if it had wings. It soared over the river and right into the central court of the crystal palace.

Rama dismounted in the shining courtyard and entered the palace. He walked through one transparent room after another until he reached the princess. She was indeed the girl he had seen in his dream.

At the same time, Amba rose from her throne in relief. "So you *are* real."

"And so are you." Rama laughed in delight and took one of his rings from a finger. "As you have given me a gift, let me give you one in return."

Putting on his ring, she took him by the hand. Together, they went back to the courtyard to Rama's horse. With another leap, the horse carried them out of the palace to the bank of the river.

When the crowd saw Rama and Amba sitting upon the horse, they began to cheer. Even the king had to admit he had made a mistake, for the two of them looked like an ideal couple.

The wedding was held shortly afterward, but Prince Rama and Princess Amba were not the only ones who got married. Their friends Luxman and Urvashi had fallen in love, as well, and so they were married at the same time. The feasting went on for days. Then Prince Rama and Princess Amba returned home with their friends, and there they lived quite contentedly for the rest of their lives.

WANDERING SOULS

In this seventeenth-century Chinese tale, a boy becomes an insect to make up for his carelessness. In Chinese mythology, there are two souls. One stays with the body to watch over it, but the other can leave. That dream soul can voyage to real places near or far away and even stranger places that lie beyond. At times, this wandering soul can slip into other bodies as easily as water poured into a jar. One can find similar beliefs among the ancient Egyptians and Africans.

The Fighting Cricket

(China)

Over five hundred years ago, there was an emperor in China who liked to watch crickets fight. Soon everyone in China imitated the emperor. The sport became so popular that a poor man named Cheng decided to catch crickets.

One day, he caught a magnificent cricket behind an old monastery. It had a powerful, long body with a dark green neck and golden wings.

When he took it home, he boasted to his wife and son, "We'll be rich soon." Then he carefully transferred the cricket to a dirt-filled pot with a lid. There he fed it a special diet of steamed crab and boiled chestnuts.

One day when Cheng was gone, his nine-year-old son, Chin, decided to play with his father's pet. But the moment he lifted the lid, the cricket escaped.

Chin chased it all around the house. Finally, with a desperate lunge, he snatched at it. However, he caught only a leg, which broke off in his hand. The poor cricket limped away and died shortly after that.

When his mother saw what Chin had done, she scolded him. "You've ruined all of your father's plans. Your father's going to give you the spanking of your life."

Chin already felt bad enough, but his mother's words scared him. So he dashed from the house. He ran until he reached the monastery and then hid behind it.

I must make it up to my father, but how? Chin asked himself. He thought and thought, but he could come up with nothing. Then, feeling tired, he lay down and fell asleep. While he slept, he felt himself leave his body like smoke from a burning log. Suddenly, he had powerful legs that let him jump over huge hills of dirt.

When he opened his eyes later, he thought it was odd how the weeds were now as tall as pagodas.

Suddenly, the ground began to shake. Turning around, Chin saw a huge mountain lumbering through the weeds. It took him a moment to realize that the mountain was his father.

In his father's arms, Chin saw his own body. His eyes were shut and his mouth was open. If he had not seen the shoulders rise and fall, he would have thought his body was dead.

Chin tried to take a step toward his father, but instead he leapt high into the air. When he landed, he looked down and saw his odd spindly legs. Quickly, he hopped over to a puddle of water and looked at his reflection. He was a small cricket with speckled wings now. But how?

His father had once explained that everybody has two souls. When people slept, one soul stayed with the body, but the dream soul left to travel to strange, faraway places. It could even enter another body.

"My dream soul must have entered another dead cricket," Chin decided. His father looked so sad that the boy tried to tell him, "Father, I'm all right." But all he could do was chirp.

Though Chin chased after his father, his leaps could not keep up with his father's long legs. Soon he was left behind.

All that evening, he traveled toward his house. Several times, he had to hide from frogs and birds and hunting insects.

He did not get home until sunrise. Wearily, he stopped before the front door. It appeared so tall now that it seemed to brush the sky.

At his insistent chirps, his father opened the door. His hair was tangled as if he had not slept all that night. Through the open doorway, Chin saw his mother. She was weeping as she kept watch beside his body.

Again, Chin tried to speak to his father, but his father simply stared blankly. Finally, in desperation, Chin leapt onto his sleeve.

His father chuckled. "I've caught many crickets, but you're the first cricket who's caught me."

Chin cringed as two towers suddenly hovered above him, until he realized it was only his father's fingers. Bravely, he let himself be plucked into the air.

"It's me," he tried to chirp. His father ignored him as he inspected the little cricket.

"You're rather small, yet you look strong and quick," Cheng said. "Maybe you're worth something after all."

Carrying his son inside, Cheng fed him a special tonic of honey and powerful herbs. Then Cheng put him into a bowl and covered it.

After taking a short nap, Chin heard a loud grating noise as the lid was lifted away. Again his father's huge hand appeared overhead. This time, though, it picked him up and put him into an empty gourd. There were holes punched in the sides so Chin could breathe.

"You're going to show me just what you're made of," his father said.

Through one of the airholes, Chin watched the countryside pass by as his father carried him. When he saw the walls of the town, Chin grew excited. They looked as tall as a mountain range. The heads of passersby seemed as large as drifting clouds. It was market day and the town square was crowded.

His father marched straight to a table covered in silk. In the center of the table was a large wide jar. In the middle of the jar was a cricket much bigger than Chin.

The referee was a skinny man who pointed to a big cricket in a fancy clay pot and announced loudly, "Who will battle Green-Gray the Mighty?" He listed the cricket's many victories. It took a very long time.

Everyone laughed when Cheng put his homely gourd on the table. The crowd would have driven Cheng away, but since no one else would risk their pets, they thought they would watch Green-Gray destroy the little cricket.

Then the referee looked at Cheng. "What is your cricket's history?"

Cheng was embarrassed after hearing all of Green-Gray's exploits, so he just put the cricket into the jar. "His name is Shrimp," he said. "And this is his first fight."

The skinny man held up his hands to stop the laughter. With a pig's bristle, he began to tickle the crickets. First he brushed their heads and then the ends of their tails and finally their big hind legs.

Green-Gray's antennae began to quiver, but Shrimp remained still as a stick. Green-Gray looked as large and as strong as a horse to him. "Father, how can I fight that monster?" he tried to chirp.

Of course, his father could not understand him. "Watch out, Shrimp. Green-Gray's going to attack," he shouted into the bowl.

Gathering his legs beneath himself, Shrimp quickly leapt over the startled head of Green-Gray. Whirling around on Green-Gray's back, he seized its neck. He would have cut off Green-Gray's head if Cheng had not taken him away. "The champ," declared the referee.

As he sat on his father's palm, Chin chirped a song of victory. Green-Gray's owner immediately wanted to buy the winner.

"I'll double the price!" another man shouted.

Chin felt proud when he heard his father announce, "I wouldn't part with this cricket for anything."

Suddenly, he heard a fluttering of wings. His night journey had made him cautious. Looking around, Chin saw a rooster land on the table. Before it could lunge, Chin leapt to the safest spot.

"Be careful where you step," his father cried.

Amused, Chin watched as the entire crowd bent over to search the ground for him. When his father finally straightened in puzzlement, he chirped, "Over here, Father."

At that now-familiar sound, his father turned and saw him clinging to the rooster's comb.

"You're as clever as you're quick," his father declared. He plucked his cricket from the rooster and stored him safely back in the gourd.

After that, Cheng cared for the cricket like a baby. When Shrimp's tiny mustache began to droop, Cheng cooled it with a fan. When Shrimp caught a cold, Cheng traveled far away to find the shoots of a green pea to feed his pet. And when Shrimp overate, Cheng fed him a special diet of red bugs.

Chin liked the attention. At first, he hesitated to eat some of the things that his father offered him. However, he soon found that his new body liked the taste.

Over the next year, Shrimp fought a hundred battles and won every one of them, until he was famous throughout the province.

His parents looked sorrowful only when they tended his real body. He would try to chirp to them not to be sad, but of course they still did not understand him.

Finally, a government clerk came to their door. "The governor has heard of your pet. He challenges it to battle his prize champion, Jade Warrior, who has defeated champions from all over the empire."

Cheng was afraid for Shrimp and replied, "I don't know if I want to risk my pet. In this short time, I've come to love him almost as much as a son."

"It is not a request. It is an order," the clerk said, then left.

"Don't worry, father." Chin tried to reassure him.

But his father could only say mournfully, "I've lost one son, and now I'm going to lose my pet."

That night before the fight, Cheng sat outside with a candle to attract the mosquitoes. When the mosquitoes had drunk their fill of his blood, he fed them to Shrimp to make his pet even fiercer.

The next day, an official escort came from the governor. Soldiers marched in front of a sedan chair. More soldiers brought up the rear.

"Take care of our son," Cheng told his wife. He got into the chair.

From inside the gourd, Chin watched the scenery pass by. The governor lived in a mansion. Servants led his father through one exquisite room after another to a garden in the rear.

There a table had been set up. Jade Warrior was a strong, magnificent creature with a handsome tail, green neck, and wings of gold. When he saw it, even Chin began to doubt.

The referee was a man dressed in a rich silk robe. After he had announced each pet's victories, he lifted up a bamboo tube with a lion on the lid. And from the tube, he took a thin blade of freshly picked crabgrass. This time, Chin decided not to wait for the usual ritual. Instead, as the referee began to tickle Jade Warrior, Chin leapt.

However, Jade Warrior was just as quick and bounded away. It was a difficult contest, with the two crickets evenly matched. They fought; they leapt. But Shrimp was quicker and smarter.

As Chin shrilled his victory song, Cheng boasted to the governor about his pet. Since the governor had witnessed Shrimp's fighting skills himself, he believed the cricket's exploits. He found it hard to believe the story about the rooster, though. "A cricket would leap away from a rooster and not toward it," he said. So he had one brought to the garden.

Instantly, Chin bounded onto the rooster's comb, where he stayed safe from harm.

"Remarkable," the governor exclaimed. "This is a pet fit for an emperor."

"Father, you can't let me go," Chin chirped in alarm.

Even if Cheng could have understood his son, there was nothing he could have done, for his father could not refuse the emperor.

So Chin was placed within a cage all of gold. When the governor had put Chin's exploits into verse, he sent both cricket and poem to the emperor.

With a sigh, Chin resolved to make the best of the trip. He had soldiers to guard him. He had servants to pamper him. When he entered the emperor's palace itself, he realized he could see sights that only princes usually see.

More determined than ever, Chin soon beat the emperor's most famous fighters, including Slick Conqueror and Green Silk.

However, Chin knew that if he was to survive, he had to do more than fight. For, he told himself, no champion lasts forever. One evening as the emperor listened to a concert, Chin danced within his cage.

"Look at how talented he is," the emperor cried in delight. He decided that Shrimp was too precious to risk in battle. After that, he took his pet everywhere with him.

The emperor was so grateful, he sent the governor horses that could race a thousand leagues without tiring. With the horses went bolts of the finest silks. The governor did not forget Cheng, either. He rewarded him with herds of horses, houses, and fifteen hundred acres of land.

Chin waited a year, until he was sure that his parents were comfortable. Then he chirped a farewell song to the emperor, whom he had come to like. And that evening, he slipped away from the cricket's body that had served him so well.

His dream soul flew back to his town in the wink of an eye. But it took him a while to find his father and mother, because they now lived in a mansion. He found them dressed in robes of silk as they knelt beside an elegant four-poster bed. On the bed lay his body. His parents were still keeping watch and tending him lovingly.

Chin darted down and slipped inside his body. It was dark for a moment. Then the boy opened his eyes. His father gasped; his mother wept with joy.

Chin told his father everything. Afterward, they heard that the emperor had gone into mourning for the cricket. As for Cheng and his son, they became two of the richest men in the empire.

LIFE IS A DREAM

Dreams are timeless. In the space of a night, we can live an entire lifetime. "South Branch" has been a popular story ever since it was written by Li Kung-tso over a thousand years ago.

South Branch

(China)

There once was a boy in China named Fen Shunyu. When Shunyu was small, his father told him, "There is glory and honor in conquering the emperor's enemy. And honor and glory are the only goals worthy of a warrior."

Shortly after that, his father rode off to fight the northern barbarians. He never came back.

So, at an early age, Shunyu vowed to be worthy of his father. When he grew up, he joined the army. He worshiped honor and glory above everything else and would do anything to gain them. Because of his many brave deeds, he was appointed an officer.

Then his company was ordered to fight the same barbarians who had killed his father. As he marched north, Shunyu vowed revenge.

The imperial army met the enemy on a high, grassy plain. In the fierce battle, there was no warrior bolder than Shunyu. And when the barbarians fled, there was no one fiercer in pursuit.

Shunyu led his soldiers high into the mountains after their foes. When the enemy retreated into a mountain pass, Shunyu ordered his troops after them. "Follow me and we will win undying glory."

However, his men held back. A wise old sergeant shook his head.

"Sir, the enemy is sure to turn that mountain pass into a death trap. If we go in, we will never come out again."

Enraged, Shunyu struck the sergeant with the flat of his sword. "Coward, where is your sense of honor?"

The sergeant endured the blows patiently. "Sir, you're young and free, so you think honor and glory are the only important things in life. But when you're older, you'll understand that there are other considerations. Most of us have wives and children. If we die in that pass, no amount of honor and glory will feed our families."

Although Shunyu beat his men and shouted himself hoarse, he could not get them to enter the pass. And so he took out his rage upon the honest sergeant. "Coward! Traitor! You aren't fit to be a soldier of the emperor—only my donkey."

"I have served you faithfully, and insults are all I get," the sergeant said, sighing. However, on the long march down to the plain, he bore Shunyu on his back without further complaint.

After they reached the army camp, the general saw Shunyu on top of the sergeant. "What are you doing to my old friend?" the general asked in astonishment.

Shunyu explained, and the general scolded him. "When I was a new officer, the sergeant gave me good counsel—advice that won battles and saved lives. Without him, I would never have lived long enough to rise to my present rank. How dare you treat him like a slave?"

Shunyu haughtily defended himself. "Because of him, the troops mutinied and the enemy escaped. I should have cut off his head."

"There is a difference between being brave and being rash," the general argued. "The sergeant saved your arrogant hide as well as your soldiers." He commanded Shunyu to apologize to the sergeant.

Shunyu refused. "Where is your sense of honor?" he said. "Where is the glory in following you? I will never apologize." And he resigned.

The proud young warrior retired to a place in the country. His favorite spot was by an ancient locust tree on the south side of his house.

Its branches intertwined like a tangle of thread. When its big yellow flowers were in fragrant bloom, Shunyu called them his lanterns.

One afternoon two friends, Cao and Xie, visited him, and they had a picnic beneath his favorite tree. "You're much too young to retire. You should beg the general to take you back," Cao urged. "A sword isn't meant to be sheathed."

"I will never apologize to the sergeant," Shunyu said loftily. Then he started to yawn because they'd just finished a big meal.

"See," Xie argued. "You're rusting away down here. The barbarians will take some of that off you."

Shunyu yawned again. "Once I've had a little rest, we'll wrestle. Then I'll show you who's rusty, my friend."

Taking off his cap, Shunyu lay down beneath the great green tree while his friends chatted with each other. Soon he was asleep.

Suddenly, Shunyu heard a polite cough. Opening his eyes, he saw two strangers standing in front of him. They wore yellow skirts and quilted jackets. Their hair bristled like boars' fur around their funny hats. Shunyu looked for his two friends, but they were nowhere in sight.

The two strangers bowed low. "We are messengers from the king of the peaceful land of Big Tree. He sends you greetings. Your reputation has reached his ears, and he begs you to come to his aid."

Shunyu had never heard of the land of Big Tree, but he assumed it was some faraway country.

"Is the cause honorable?" Shunyu asked, for his friends' visit had made him restless for adventure.

"It is," they assured him.

"Then, as I love honor above life, I'll help."

Shunyu got up and saw a small, bright green chariot. It was drawn by four horses impatiently pawing the ground. On either side was an escort of eight warriors in black quilted coats.

Eagerly, Shunyu climbed into the chariot with the royal messengers. The first messenger took the reins and sent the chariot rattling along at a fast clip while the soldiers fell in behind them. To Shunyu's surprise, the messenger turned the chariot toward the locust tree.

"Watch out!" Shunyu shouted. "We're going to crash."

Just as Shunyu cried out, the tree seemed to swell till it filled the sky. The chariot hurtled through a hole at the base of the tree and then into the tree itself. Shunyu was too stunned to ask questions. Instead, he gripped the chariot's side as it swept on. In back of him, his escort kept the same urgent pace.

The chariot whizzed past strange trees. It hurried across slow-moving rivers of sticky amber fluid and over odd, twisting hills. Soon the men came to a huge city surrounded by great walls and towers. An endless stream of people and carts flowed in and out of the gates and through the streets.

With a further burst of speed, the escorting soldiers raced to clear a path. "Make way!" they shouted.

Instantly, the carts and people drew to either side. With the soldiers leading the way, Shunyu and his companions reached the inner city. Above the gate hung a huge sign announcing THE PEACE OF BIG TREE.

As they clattered through the front gate, a guard saluted Shunyu. A mounted officer rode up to greet the new arrivals. "I am to lead you to the Hall of the East Flower."

The chariot followed the officer to a gate that suddenly swung open. The officer jumped off his horse and motioned Shunyu toward a hall with delicately carved columns and brightly painted railings. Inside, there were miniature trees in pots and bowls of every sort of rare fruit. Though Shunyu had traveled a good deal in his adventures, he did not recognize any of them. Ornate tables and chairs and stools filled the hall, and brocade curtains covered the walls. Tables groaned with all kinds of treats to drink and eat.

Shunyu paced back and forth restlessly. Finally, a man with an ivory scepter and purple-red robes entered. He introduced himself as the chancellor and led Shunyu through a set of scarlet gates into a huge hall, where a tall, noble-looking man sat upon a throne. Though he was dressed in a robe of plain white silk, he wore a ruby crown upon his head. Here is a ruler worthy of my service, Shunyu thought to himself.

And Shunyu gladly knelt and bowed so low that his forehead touched the floor.

"Fen Shunyu," the king said solemnly, "we thank heaven that you have arrived at last. Every day, things grow worse in the province of South Branch. Its soil was fertile. Its people were happy, and for a long time, they were content to be in our care. Recently, however, certain evil people have been stirring up trouble. Now the fields are empty. Will you bring peace to that unhappy land so that it may blossom again?"

Shunyu bowed respectfully. "I'm a rough soldier who knows nothing about diplomacy."

"You have a brave heart and should have been appreciated long ago," the king insisted. He pressed Shunyu until the warrior finally accepted the post.

The next morning, Shunyu set off with some troops for South Branch. After a day's journey, he crossed its border. Weeds grew in the fields, and the villages were deserted. As he passed the ruined towns, Shunyu said to himself, If I am going to win honor and glory here, it will not be enough to win battles. I must restore prosperity to the land.

As soon as he could, Shunyu marched out from the capital of South Branch with a small band of soldiers. On a plain outside the city, the rebels attacked him, but with his courage and superior tactics, Shunyu defeated them in one swift, decisive battle.

Shunyu returned to his palace in the capital and set himself to study the land's problems. He began an ambitious program to build more dams and canals. People returned to their ruined fields and even cleared more land to plant crops. Soon the land was at peace as it had once been.

In gratitude, the king made him governor of South Branch and gave him the hand of his second daughter, the princess of the Golden Stem.

Shunyu served as governor for twenty years, and the people had never been wealthier or more at peace. There were many popular songs praising him. And at their own expense, people erected monuments in his honor.

The king could not have been more pleased. To Shunyu, the king gave all the tax money from an entire city. And he raised Shunyu to the highest noble rank. When the old chancellor finally died, the king named Shunyu as his successor.

Shunyu and the princess had seven children, five boys and two girls, who themselves married members of other royal families. No one in the kingdom of Big Tree had ever risen faster or higher. Shunyu had won more glory than he had ever hoped for. He just wished his father could have seen him.

Shunyu's popularity did not go unnoticed, however. The old aristocracy resented the meteoric rise of a newcomer and began to whisper lies and slander to the king. "The foreigner wants to become king himself," they said. And as they poured poison into the ear of the king, he gradually grew afraid of losing his throne.

Then an abscess developed on the back of the princess. In less than ten days, she died.

Overwhelmed by grief, Shunyu remembered what his old sergeant had said. "The sergeant was right. I would trade all my honors to bring my love back again."

The princess was buried in a special place called Dragon Tongue Hill. As Shunyu led the funeral procession, the people of Big Tree streamed from their homes to wail and lament. Nobles and commoners alike came to mourn the princess and honor Shunyu.

"You see," his enemies whispered to the king. "Now the foreigner is even more popular than you."

At that, the frightened king finally turned against Shunyu. He stripped Shunyu of his wealth and servants and bodyguard, and sent him to live in the stable and look after the horses.

Shunyu said, "Now I know how the sergeant felt when I humiliated him. I'll suffer it just as bravely as he did." His one consolation was his grandchildren, who often came to visit him. "They are worth far more than mere honor and glory," he said. "If I were ordered into a mountain pass, I would not go, either."

Soon his enemies ended even that pleasure. They forbade the grandchildren to see Shunyu.

Shunyu had borne the loss of his wife bravely, and he had not complained when all his possessions had been taken away. However, this was the final humiliation. One afternoon, when the king came to ride his horses, Shunyu cried out to him, "What evil have I done to you, Your Highness? All I've done is serve you as well and as faithfully as I could."

"It is a shame," the king said coldly, "that my daughter has died. But now you have no ties here. You should return to your home."

"After all these years of loyal service, this is my home," Shunyu declared.

"This can never be your real home," the king replied.

Shunyu began to weep. "So this is how the quest for honor and glory ends. I might as well have tried to grasp the morning mist. All right, I'll go."

The next morning, the two messengers who had first brought him appeared to escort Shunyu out of Big Tree. However, their robes and caps seemed a little ragged, and their hair unkempt, as if they, too, had fallen from favor.

They led him through a great doorway and out of the palace. This time, instead of a swift chariot, there was only a broken-down oxcart that rumbled slowly along. It seemed to feel every hole and rock on the road. "How much longer?" Shunyu asked.

But the two messengers were now as rude as they had once been polite. They ignored him and began to sing in a bored way. It was only much later that one of them said, "We can dump him soon."

A moment later, the oxcart rolled through the hole in the old locust tree and Shunyu saw his old home. As he fought back tears, he felt himself overwhelmed by homesickness.

When he climbed out of the cart, he saw himself asleep in the shade of the tree. Stunned, he could only stand there. Then he felt his eyelids draw up like shutters, and he woke from his dream to find himself lying down. Above him, he saw the green-topped tree. When he sat up, the oxcart was gone, and the sun was setting.

"But on what day and what year?" he asked as he walked cautiously toward the house. He was not sure who lived there now.

Shunyu saw one of his servants sweeping the steps with a broom. "Are you done, master? I'll bring the lunch things in."

In an inner courtyard, he saw his friends with their feet in a tub of water. "How was your nap, old man?" they teased. "Feel any better?"

"What day and what year is it?" Shunyu demanded.

The two friends glanced at each other. "Maybe you'd better take another nap."

Shunyu grabbed Cao by his collar. "Tell me."

"What's gotten into you?" the startled man asked. "We left you napping under the tree just a few hours ago."

"It's the same day?" Shunyu asked.

"Of course," Cao said, as if Shunyu had taken leave of his senses. He stared at his friend when Shunyu called for an ax and took them back to the locust tree.

He showed them the hole he had dreamed about. Then Shunyu took the ax and chopped at the roots until he revealed a mound of dirt shaped like a city. Ants swarmed all around. "This looks like the royal capital of Big Tree," Shunyu gasped.

A little distance away, they found a small pile of dirt that curved like a dragon's tongue. "This is where the princess is buried." The ax fell from Shunyu's stunned fingers. "I have lived a lifetime in the space of a few hours."

When he told his friend the whole story, they would have burned the tree down. But Shunyu would not let them. Instead, he covered up the holes he had made in the tree.

That night, a big storm arrived, so strong that it blew the very tiles from the roof. When the sun came out the next day, Shunyu went to check on the ants, but they were all gone.

Sadder and wiser, Shunyu gave away his horses and his arms. When his friends asked him why, he said, "My father was wrong, and the sergeant was right. There is more to life than honor and glory. I had all that anyone could want. And in the end, honor and glory brought only sorrow and shame."

People who met Shunyu now did not recognize him. Instead of the brash, hot-blooded warrior, Shunyu had become courteous. When he spoke, it was with care and after deep thought.

In time people sought out Shunyu for his wisdom, so that he became more famous than he ever had been as a warrior. And though he himself did not care one bit about his new reputation, his modesty only increased his fame.

DREAMS HEAL

It is believed in many societies that dreams can heal.
In ancient Greece, the god Asclepius would enter a patient's dream
and analyze clues to an illness. The next morning, the patient would
tell the dream to the priests at the temple of Asclepius. The priests, in turn,
would interpret the dream and prescribe what the dreamer needed to do to get well.
The Chinese have their own god of medicine. However, in this story
Li Ming-Chung's illness is cured by one of the gods who protects the home,
and the cure is far more immediate than the ones provided in the
temple of Asclepius. His case was recorded nine centuries ago in China.

The Rescue

(China)

There was once a man named Li Ming-Chung who sought a job with the government. Though he passed the lower exams, Ming-Chung failed to pass the higher ones, so he had neither employment nor the money that came with it. He decided to move with his wife and his mother to the country, where living was cheap.

Ming-Chung earned a little money by painting portraits and writing letters for people. Although his wife and mother were happy enough, he only felt sorry for himself. Then one day, a man in a distant village commissioned him to paint a portrait.

"I wish you wouldn't go so far," his wife said.

"If I stay in this mud hole, how am I going to buy food?" Ming-Chung asked sourly as he packed his things.

"Go then if you must," his mother said. She presented him with a meal wrapped in a cloth. "But if you meet a crooked man, be polite."

"I'm always polite," Ming-Chung said brusquely. Before he could head out the door, his mother pulled him over to the humble little shrine. "It won't hurt to ask the spirits of our home to protect you on your trip."

Lighting the incense, she stuck it into a cup of dirt and began to pray. Ming-Chung grumbled to the picture of the god of the house, "I don't know why I should ask you for help. The spirit of this old pile couldn't do much." And he made his escape quickly.

Ming-Chung walked briskly away from their home. His wife and mother stood in the doorway to wave, but he did not even turn around. Instead, he took long, impatient strides that carried him swiftly along the winding road. They took him deep into the mountains, past sharp-edged cliffs and peaks pointed like daggers.

Ming-Chung did not stop until he reached a tiny hamlet where fields ran in terraces up the mountainsides and the stench of goats and sheep filled the air. Here he met the leader of the hamlet, who wanted his portrait painted for future generations. He was wearing an old moth-eaten robe that had gone out of fashion two generations ago. "Where were you? I've been waiting hours."

"I'm sorry. It took longer to walk here than I thought," Ming-Chung said, and hurriedly set to mixing his paints.

It took most of the day, but the leader was pleased with his painting. As soon as he was paid, Ming-Chung left. Though mountains had already hidden the setting sun, he could see the sky above the peaks changing from red to purple and then to deepest black. Faintly on the horizon, he could see lights twinkling like stars. As he surveyed them, he wondered which might be his home.

From behind him, he could smell supper cooking in the tiny houses of the hamlet, and he remembered the meal his mother had wrapped for him. He did not stop for his meal, but ate as he walked. It was growing dark and he had far to go.

"That smells wonderful," an old man said in a quavery voice.

Ming-Chung turned around to see a man with bent legs and arms and back. Even his nose was crooked, and his hair twisted this way and that. "I'm so very hungry," the crooked man said. His voice rose high and then low as if it were bent, too. "I don't suppose you could spare a bite to eat?"

Ming-Chung was so annoyed that he forgot his mother's warning. He snapped, "No. I have only enough for myself."

The old man's voice cracked as he laughed. "You should be civil when you're far away from home."

"Go and beg back there." Ming-Chung nodded toward the hamlet. "They have plenty of food."

"They're not using my road," the crooked man said.

"You're not eating my food," Ming-Chung said, and he took a bite. Brushing past the crooked man, he walked on. A little while later, he could barely see the road at all. On either side, the trees and strange rocks loomed like monsters.

The crooked man had followed Ming-Chung. Hobbling up on a twisted staff, he asked, "Have you got anything left?"

"No. Now leave me alone." Ming-Chung hurried on.

Soon, though, it was too dark to eat. Overhead, the stars wheeled across the sky like an army of fireflies, but everything else was as black as his inks. Ming-Chung had to concentrate on each step, shuffling forward and feeling for the road with his toes.

After a few minutes, the crooked man appeared at Ming-Chung's elbow, his bald head gleaming like a big broad turnip in the faint star-light. "It's very rude to leave without sharing," he said.

"I told you to go away." Ming-Chung tried to shove the old man away from him.

However, the old man was more nimble than he looked. He easily dodged Ming-Chung, saying, "You asked for it." With his staff, he tripped the young man.

Frightened, Ming-Chung felt himself fall down the mountainside.

The wind rushed by his ears. In a panic, he tried to clutch at something—anything—that could break his fall.

Suddenly, he landed on a ledge. His head struck a rock so hard that he nearly bit his tongue. As Ming-Chung lay there looking up at the stars, his first thought was that he was alive. His second thought was whether he had broken anything. Carefully, he felt himself all over, but he was fine.

He got to his feet slowly. Though he had lost his meal and his paints, he decided to travel on. He could come back tomorrow and look for them in the daylight.

In the darkness, Ming-Chung inched his way along the ledge and found that it joined the path again. Though it had been hard to move at first, he found it got easier with each step. He had not gone very far before the moon began to rise. In its cold, frosty light, he realized that he had reached the foothills.

He hiked ten kilometers before he saw his home and garden. He smiled when he saw the vines his wife had planted. She was so proud of her string beans. In the moonlight, house and garden looked as if they had been cast in silver.

"I've seen mansions in the capital that aren't half as nice as our home." He wondered out loud, "Why didn't I notice this before? I should paint it."

Ming-Chung went inside eagerly. There, next to a lantern, his mother sat embroidering while his wife worked a small hand loom. They were so busy that they didn't look up, so he went over to his mother.

"I'm so glad to be home," he said to her.

When his mother didn't answer, he figured that she was trying to concentrate on some difficult stitch. Going over to his wife, he called loudly over the clacking of the loom, "You won't believe what happened to me." When she still ignored him, he tried to touch her elbow. "I've got some money. Tomorrow, let's buy some pork and have a little celebration."

However, his wife went on weaving as if she had heard nothing.

"What's wrong with you?" he complained. "I'm talking to you."

However, no matter how loudly he shouted or how hard he tried to get their attention, he might have been just a gnat flitting about.

Finally, his mother looked over at his wife. "He's very late. I hope nothing's happened."

His wife paused in her work. "Maybe we should look for him."

His mother was silent for a moment. "Let's give him a little while longer. He'd be very cross if he thought we were fussing too much."

With a nod, his wife went back to her weaving and his mother returned to her embroidery.

Frightened now, Ming-Chung held out his arms to them. "But I'm here."

Suddenly from overhead, he heard a polite cough. When he looked up at the roof rafters, he saw a little old man with a long gray goatee and a few wisps of hair on his head.

Ming-Chung's jaw dropped open. "Who are you?"

The little old man hopped nimbly to the floor. "No time for introductions. We have to get you back to your body."

"But I'm right here," Ming-Chung began to protest.

"Only one of your souls is here," the little old man said. Taking Ming-Chung's hand, he began to pull him along. "You're still dreaming. The fall knocked one of your souls loose and it came here. But your body is still back where you left it. The spirit of the mountain road is abusing it even now while you dream. If we don't get you reunited soon, you'll die."

"Stop," Ming-Chung cried as the little old man dragged him straight toward the wall.

"No time, no time." And the little old man yanked him right through the wall with a pop.

The moon was climbing through the sky like a cold, pale disk. On its face, Ming-Chung thought he saw the woman on the moon. The woman's face seemed chiseled into the surface like a stone seal.

Ming-Chung was bubbling over with questions for the little old man. "Was the crooked man the spirit of the mountain road?"

"No time, no time," the little man insisted anxiously. Though his legs were short, he moved them very fast. It was all Ming-Chung could do to keep up with him.

They made their way back to the foot of the mountains. There on a ledge, they found Ming-Chung's body lying among the rocks as it dreamed. The crooked old man stood over it. Leaning on his staff, he kicked Ming-Chung in the ribs.

"Excuse me, sir," the little man called to the crooked man. "In his haste to get home, the young man forgot to give you this." The little man picked up the remains of Ming-Chung's meal, which was still wrapped in the cloth.

The crooked man held out a gnarled palm. "Next time, he should remember who owns this road."

As soon as the little man gave him the food, the crooked man vanished. Letting go of Ming-Chung's hand, the little man went to his body and hoisted it into a sitting position. "Li Ming-Chung," he called formally, "come back."

And Ming-Chung felt himself being drawn back to his body. As he slipped inside, he asked the little man, "Who are you?"

The little man smiled sourly. "The spirit of the 'old pile.'"

"I'm sorry I didn't recognize you," Ming-Chung said, for he saw now that the little man looked like the picture in the shrine at home. "Thank you. You were kind to rescue me."

"I didn't do it for you," the little man sniffed. "It was for your mother. She's always been nice to me."

For a moment, Ming-Chung felt dizzy, as if he were seeing with two pairs of eyes. So he shut them. When he raised his eyelids again, he felt as groggy as if he had just awakened. He was sitting on the cold, hard stones, but the little man had vanished. Ming-Chung felt his limbs and found that nothing was broken, although his ribs were sore.

Seeing his pouch of paints, Ming-Chung picked it up. The moon shone upon the road, turning it into a gleaming, silvery ribbon. Frightened, he hurried home, but he did not get there until the early morning hours.

In his haste, he tried to go right through the door as he had gone through the wall before. But this time he had a body, so he banged right into it. When his mother opened the door, she held out a lantern. "What's all that racket? Oh, it's you."

"Thank heaven," his wife said fervently. "We were so worried about you." She was dressed to go out, as was his mother.

His mother held up the lantern to examine his cuts and scrapes and bruises. "What happened to you? Did you fall off the mountain?"

"I'll explain in a moment. First, I have to do something else." Ming-Chung borrowed the lantern so he could light an incense stick and thank the spirit of their home. Afterward, he told his wife and mother about his adventures while he cleaned his wounds.

When he was recovered, he began taking walks with his family. As he scrambled about, he found various minerals and plants with which to make vivid paints. Then, at home, Ming-Chung painted vast landscapes on scrolls that covered three walls: huge craggy mountains, forests of a blue-green that made your heart ache, skies that seemed to stretch up to heaven. Tucked away at the foot of the mountains were his cozy home, his mother, his wife, and himself—just as he had seen them on that strange evening.

Soon after that, wealthy collectors began to buy Ming-Chung's paintings. Though he became rich enough to leave the little cottage and move to a mansion in the capital, he stayed right where he was. Every night, the spirit of that little cottage had his sweet incense and his own little snack, as well.

And on all their walks, Ming-Chung and his family always brought along a meal wrapped in cloth—just in case they met the crooked man.

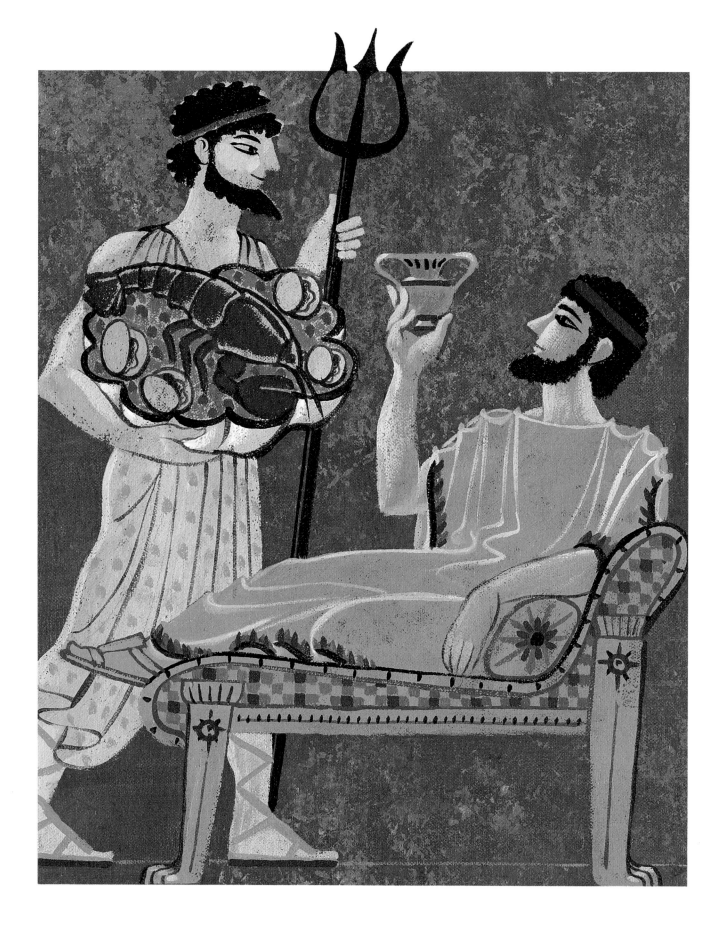

THE PRICE OF A DREAM

*Dreams bring heartache, sometimes, because anything is possible
in a dream: wealth, success, the return of a loved one.
At night, dreams can grant whatever we wish for.
But in the morning, there is always a little sadness when we realize that our
dreams are not real. It is an intimately human feeling.
Here is an ancient Greek tale in which a judge sets a poetic price
upon that bittersweet experience.*

Paying with Shadows

(Greece)

Over two thousand years ago, there was a city in Egypt called Alexandria. In that city, there lived a Greek woman named Thonis who was famous for her cooking. She would go to the mansions of rich people and prepare fabulous feasts. Everything had to be perfect. The dates had to be the freshest, the larks had to be the fattest, and the wines had to be the rarest.

One man, famous for his taste buds, sampled her fish sauce. After one taste, he sighed and said now he could die because he would never have any better.

Thonis took her own pots and pans to a mansion, for she trusted no one else's equipment. And she allowed neither dancers nor musicians nor acrobats to entertain at the feast—her food was the main attraction.

Thonis had been born a slave, yet she had always wanted to be free. So she watched everything the head cook did. When she thought she had learned enough, she offered to help, and the head cook let her.

Gradually, Thonis learned everything there was to know about cooking. When she started cooking for her master and his guests, she dazzled them with her dishes. Where artists used paints, Thonis used sauces. Where sculptors used chisels, she used her knives.

Her master and his friends were so pleased that they sent her gifts of money. Instead of spending it, she saved every coin. Eventually, Thonis had enough to buy her freedom.

Once she was free, Thonis soon had all the rich folk in Alexandria begging her to cook for them. She kept charging them more and more, and to her amusement, they kept paying. Thonis herself was not greedy. She lived and dressed simply. "I don't care about money," she liked to say. "But money means I can do what I want. And what I want to do is cook."

Her customers had to make appointments months in advance. Although Thonis cooked almost every night, only a few got to sample her cooking at any one time. Those few counted themselves among the most fortunate in all Alexandria, for they had tasted Thonis's artistry.

In that same city, there was a certain rich man named Aristobolos. As a boy, he had gone to sea and then had worked his way up to captain. He had sailed far and wide and had become rich, for no one else could bring back spices and silks as he could. Aristobolos bought ship after ship, until his fleet roamed the seven seas.

Though his face remained tough as leather from years in the sun and his hands remained calloused from decades of hauling on ships' ropes, he was so wealthy that he no longer saw his old friends and shipmates.

Instead, he gave dinner parties for other rich people. Some of them accepted, but many did not. That hurt and puzzled Aristobolos. "Why won't they come? No one ever walked away hungry from one of my parties."

His steward coughed politely and explained, "I'm afraid your fare isn't fancy enough. People are saying you're stingy. But that would stop if you had Thonis cook for you."

Aristobolos was sensitive about his reputation. He knew many people still looked down upon him for his humble origins. "I'll show them."

So he dutifully asked Thonis to make one of her meals for him and his friends. She told him he would have to wait six months. Now, Aristobolos was a master of many ships. He had the ear of Ptolemy, the ruler of Egypt, and could see him whenever he wanted. He was not used to waiting for anyone. He offered to double her usual fee if she would cook for him that night.

However, Thonis insisted she could not disappoint the other people on her waiting list. If Aristobolos didn't like it, he could simply go somewhere else.

Aristobolos squirmed. No one had talked to him like that since he had been a cabin boy many years ago. He remembered what his steward had said: People were talking. He had to have Thonis as his chef.

"Very well," he said through gritted teeth. "But spare no expense. I want you to cook the finest banquet you ever have."

"I'll cook what I please," she answered, "and you'll like it or not. I don't care. I don't cook for just anyone."

Swallowing his pride, Aristobolos forced himself to say that he understood and accepted.

Thonis nodded. "Very well. You may invite no more than eleven other guests. And I won't have entertainers distracting people from my meals. You'll have good food and good wine. And if you have any wit, you'll have good conversation."

Aristobolos retreated to his mansion and let people know he had engaged Thonis six months in advance. He would send invitations only to a few select friends.

Suddenly, his rich acquaintances fawned over him. Haughty nobles who had once snubbed him, now said pleasant things to him. Aristobolos liked the attention he got because he planned to host a Thonis feast. He felt as if he had finally arrived in society.

For almost six months, Aristobolos enjoyed himself. If people displeased him, he would tease them and threaten to strike their names from the list. Because he was having such fun, he postponed sending his invitations to the last possible moment. Eventually, on the eve of the banquet, he had made his choices, delighting a few and disappointing many. Then he went to bed, anticipating the feast the next evening.

That night, though, he dreamed he was all alone on his dining couch. Diana, the goddess of the hunt, came to him, holding out a silver crescent-tipped arrow. It had been thrust through a pastry in the shape of an egg. "From Thonis," she said.

When he cracked open the pastry egg, he found a spiced quail baked inside and he gobbled it down. The meat melted in his mouth.

Then Neptune, the god of the sea, carried in a huge seashell. "From Thonis," he rumbled, setting it before Arisotobolos. From it, he took lobsters and clams cooked in Thonis's fish sauce. They reminded him of spicy winds from distant shores.

Each dish was more exquisite than the last, and the wines reminded him of the remote places he had visited—frosty Thule and sunny Serai. Because it was a dream, he never felt too hungry or too full.

He was sorry when he woke up the next morning and his dream banquet came to an end. As he lay in bed, he realized that all the fun had gone out of the scheduled feast. As good a chef as Thonis was, she could never make a meal to match the one she had cooked in his dream.

You've turned into a donkey, he told himself. Where were all these friends when you were poor and needed help? Why worry about impressing those geese? Last night, you tasted paradise. Why spoil it?

And so he sent a note to Thonis telling her not to come that night. He also explained why.

Thonis was annoyed when she received the note. However, she did not lose any money. Even on such short notice, there were many rich people happy to have her cook one of her banquets.

Still, the more Thonis thought about it, the more worried she became. She had not gained her freedom by letting the rich trick her.

Besides, what if her other customers started dreaming such banquets, as well? If she had cooked a meal in his dream, she ought to be paid. So she sued Aristobolos.

For months, the city talked of nothing but that particular case. Everyone took one side or the other. Philosophers argued. Lawyers got into fistfights. When the day of the trial came, all of Alexandria packed the court. Thonis got up and presented her side of the argument. Then Aristobolos got up and told his version. He couldn't help going into loving detail about the feast with many smacks of his lips.

When they were both done, the judge, Bocchoris, ordered Aristobolos to fill a vase with gold coins. Then he ordered Thonis to hold out her hands with her palms upward. Everyone thought the judge would tell Aristobolos to pour gold into her two hands.

Instead, the judge commanded Aristobolos to move the vase in a certain way. When Aristobolos did, the shadow of the gold moved over Thonis's hands. As soon as Aristobolos was finished, the judge declared, "For dreams, a person pays and is paid with shadows."

And so the trial came to an end. Thonis was angry and afraid at first, but she found she was even more in demand than before. Now everyone wanted the "dream feast" of Aristobolos. To everyone's delight, the challenge made Thonis rise to new heights of the cooking arts. However, after that, Thonis added another condition to her services. She was to be paid even if someone only dreamed of a meal she cooked.

As for Aristobolos, he gave up on fancy cuisine and went back to the plain, simple meals of his youth. He always maintained that nothing would match the meal he'd had in his dreams. Instead of the rich folk, he invited his old friends and shipmates to dine on sausages and bread and goat cheese and onions. They spent long hours telling tall tales and reminiscing about the old days. And Aristobolos found that the good company and conversation made the simple fare taste as good as one of Thonis's banquets.

THE HUNGER FOR DREAMS

Almost every culture has a story in which the dreamer receives secret instructions from a saint, a spirit, or a deity. The knowledge can be something hidden from ordinary people or something lost over the ages. In either case, it is a special dreamer who receives this lore. Here is a South American story that presents the theme with a twist, for the visions and dreams themselves can become addictive.

The Dream Tree

(Brazil)

There once was a boy named Uaicá who was picked on by the other boys. Though his grandfather tried to protect him, he could not be with him all the time. Uaicá's only escape was to go into the rain forest. He liked to walk beneath the tall trees whose leafy, green tops waved far overhead. High above, he saw splashes of color—flowering vines that wound themselves around the tree trunks like snakes.

One day as Uaicá was busy gazing upward, he stumbled over a sleeping tapir. The creature lay upon its belly, with its curling snout in the dirt. Next to it was a sloth with long, curving claws to grasp tree branches. Beyond them were wild pigs and otters and deer and monkeys, and even an alligator and a long anaconda. All of them were fast asleep beneath a strange tree that Uaicá had never seen before.

Curious, he picked his way through the animals to the tree itself. As he began to examine it, he felt himself grow drowsy. His jaw stretched wide in a bone-cracking yawn. He tried to turn and leave, but his legs were like rubber. As soon as Uaicá hit the ground, he was asleep, too.

Soon he began to dream. He saw many different animals. Some he recognized; others he did not. He dreamed of his friends and family and also of people he did not know. When these strangers sang, Uaicá listened.

Then, in his dream, he met a pale, wrinkled man. "I am Sinaá," the old man said, "the child of the jaguar."

Sinaá told him many things. He described the time that he stole fire from the eagle and how he made all the tasty food plants from the ashes of a dead snake. He even explained how he had once owned the dark night—when there had been only daytime in the world.

When Uaicá finally woke, the sun had already set. In the gray twilight, he saw he was alone. All the animals had awakened and left. Quickly, he ran home through the darkening forest.

The next morning before breakfast, Uaicá made his way back to the tree. He was curious and wanted to see more. Walking up to the tree, he suddenly felt tired again and fell down on the ground.

Uaicá soon found himself in the dream world. Once more he saw the animals and heard the strange people singing. Sinaá also came to talk to him again. And just as he had the day before, Uaicá woke at sunset.

Too excited to eat dinner, he was back the next day to dream again. Because he left at sunrise, before breakfast, and returned home when it was too late to eat, Uaicá ate nothing for several days.

At last, Sinaá noticed how thin Uaicá was getting. "You have seen quite a lot of my world, but you must never come back. If you visit me once more, you might never leave."

Back in the village, Uaicá's grandfather had also noticed how skinny his grandson was. He had saved some food for Uaicá. When Uaicá came home that evening, he ate hungrily.

As Uaicá wolfed down his food, his grandfather said, "You leave before the food's ready in the morning and you come home when there's no food left. Where do you go in the forest?"

Eagerly, Uaicá shared his secret with his grandfather. Naturally, his grandfather wanted to visit the dream tree, too, so Uaicá took him. However, with Sinaá's words fresh in his memory, Uaicá stopped a safe distance from the tree. "Walk under that tree," he told his grandfather, "and your journey will begin."

As soon as his grandfather reached the tree, he fell to the ground and began snoring. As Uaicá kept watch over his grandfather, animals drifted up to the tree and fell asleep next to the old man.

It was hard for Uaicá to sit there while his grandfather and all the animals were dreaming. He was tempted to join his grandfather in the dream world. Surely one last trip wouldn't hurt. But then he remembered Sinaá's warning. He realized one more visit might keep him in that dream world forever, so he stayed where he was.

His grandfather woke up a short while later. He seemed very upset. Rubbing his head, he walked around the sleeping animals and joined Uaicá.

"Did you dream anything?" Uaicá asked, puzzled.

Still looking disturbed, his grandfather shook his head. "Only a little, and I didn't like what I dreamed."

"Did you meet Sinaá?" Uaicá asked.

His grandfather wouldn't tell him. "I don't think you should tell anyone else about the dream tree," he said. "It's not a good thing to go there."

So Uaicá promised his grandfather he would tell no one else. That afternoon when they returned home, Uaicá discovered that the cruelest of all the bullies, a boy named Xibute, had fallen ill. His family had tried everything to make him well, but nothing had worked.

However, Sinaá had shown Uaicá how to heal sickness. Slowly, Uaicá made his way past the weeping family to Xibute's hammock. Putting his hand on the boy, Uaicá took the illness away.

Everyone was astounded. They had never imagined that Uaicá had any sort of power. Soon, sick people from all around came to see the boy

THE HUNGER FOR DREAMS

they had once ignored. Those who could not walk were carried. With a mere touch, Uaicá healed them all.

Then one night, as Uaicá lay in his hammock, he dreamed he met Sinaá again. "You passed the greatest tests. You were strong enough to stay away from the dream tree, and you were kind enough to heal your enemy. Now I will teach you my powers so you can take care of our people as I once did."

That night and every night thereafter, Uaicá visited Sinaá in the dream world. He did not have to go to the tree anymore to learn Sinaá's wisdom. And he used Sinaá's secrets only for good.

His grandfather built a house for Uaicá where he could dream his special dreams. In the garden, they grew special plants. And Xibute became Uaicá's friend and helper. He moved in with Uaicá and his grandfather.

During one visit to the dream world, Uaicá saw a handsome necklace. "Grandfather would like this," he said, picking it up. Then he noticed another. "And Xibute would like that." So he got that one also.

When he woke, Uaicá gave the necklaces to his grandfather and Xibute. They were both delighted with their presents. After that, Uaicá began to bring other things from the dream world for his grandfather and his friend.

Soon, though, the rest of the tribe noticed the necklaces and other gifts. They asked Uaicá's grandfather where they had come from, but the grandfather was wise and would not tell. So the tribe asked Xibute. The young man was happy to talk, for he did not know any better.

"Uaicá brings these gifts back from the dream world," Xibute explained.

As soon as they heard that, the tribe became jealous. Soon everyone clamored for presents. They hounded Uaicá all day.

At last, Uaicá became so exasperated that he scolded them. "I can't spend all my time hunting for gifts for the whole tribe. I go to the dream world to learn things to help you."

His grandfather thought he could make peace. "So you won't be envious, Uaicá will take back his gifts and leave them in the dream world." And his grandfather returned his necklace and his other presents to Uaicá. Xibute did, too.

That only made the tribe angrier. Some of the boys who had once bullied Uaicá gathered together to complain. "Now he thinks he's so much better than we are," they grumbled. They decided to kill Uaicá. "But how?" they asked one another.

Finally, one of them had an idea. "Let's wait till he's eating. He'll be so busy, we'll be able to surprise him."

They hid near Uaicá's house. Toward late afternoon, Uaicá returned with his grandfather and Xibute. In their hands, they had fish freshly caught from the river.

The boys waited while Uaicá cooked the fish. When he sat down to eat with his grandfather and Xibute, his enemies crept out of the bushes as if they were stalking tapirs. The quietest one sneaked up behind Uaicá's back. As he raised his club, Uaicá put down his fish. "I have learned many things in the dream world. I can even see without turning around," he said.

Quickly, one boy brought the club down. But Uaicá was quick as the wind. He slipped off the stool and vanished into the earth. In that instant, his house, his grandfather, Xibute, and everything they owned winked out of sight. His enemies were left alone in an empty dirt field.

Uaicá took his grandfather and Xibute and all their belongings far under the ground. Then he brought them up again to the surface, far away from his attackers. There he went on dreaming and learning from Sinaá.

Frantically, the elders of the tribe looked for Uaicá, for no one else had his powers of healing. Unknowingly, they sent a party of Uaicá's enemies to search through the jungle and in the mountains and along the river. After a long while, they located him far away.

"Go away," his grandfather said. "How dare you come here!"

Uaicá, however, acted as if nothing had happened. "It's always nice for friends to visit," he said.

Uaicá's enemies pretended to be sorry. "Won't you come back?" they begged. "The tribe needs you."

Uaicá let his enemies talk him into returning to his village. The tribe was overjoyed. For a little while, his enemies pretended to be happy, too.

One day, though, his enemies went down to the river and caught many fish. Then some of them told Uaicá, "You've done so much for us that we want to give a feast in your honor."

When the feast was ready, they set a stool on the ground and told Uaicá to sit. As he began to eat his fish, one of his enemies crept up behind him with a club.

Again, Uaicá knew what the killer was doing, even though his back was to the boy. As the club descended, Uaicá slipped away. This time, the club cracked a big rock on the ground. Uaicá, his grandfather, Xibute, and all their belongings disappeared into the crevice.

Before he left, Uaicá said to his enemies, "I will never return. You don't deserve to know the many things Sinaá has taught me." With that, Uaicá vanished. And with him went the lessons of the dream world.

To this day, the tribe says Uaicá dreams inside the rock with his grandfather and Xibute. In their dreams, they listen to Sinaá as he teaches them all the wonderful secrets that have been lost over the years. And though the tribe searched all over the forest for the dream tree, no one has ever found it.

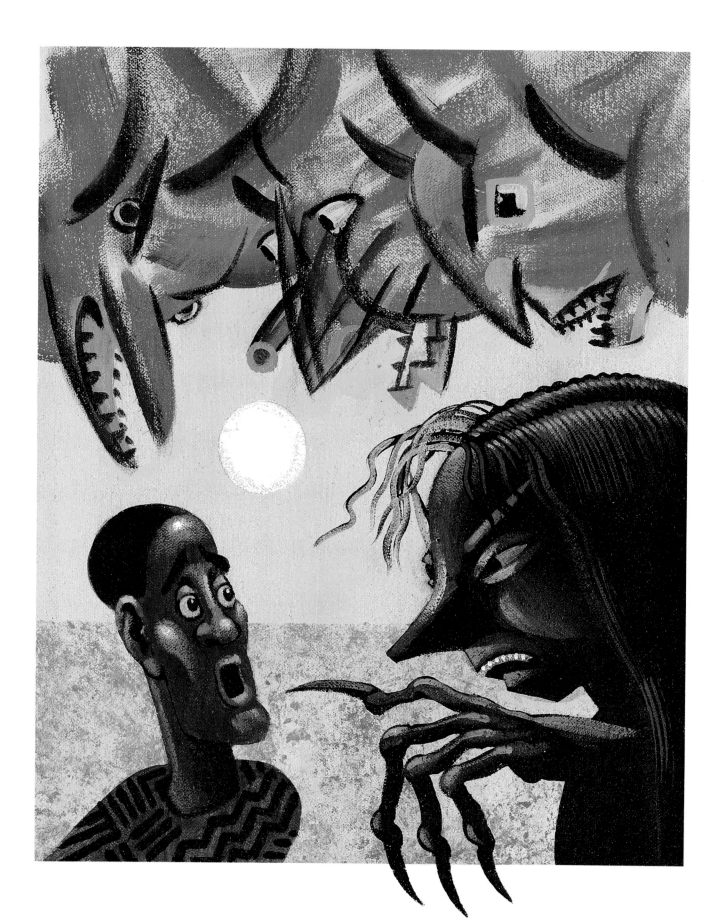

DREAMS AND CREATIVITY

*There has always been a close relationship between dreams and
creativity. Many writers and artists have drawn inspiration from
their dreams. Mary Shelley, for example, said that her novel
Frankenstein originated with a dream.
Here is an African tale in which a dream provides the creative spark.
In Senegal, the Tukolor weavers entwine more than threads.
They also weave words into poems and songs. According to
Professor Roy M. Dilley, weavers and magic are intimately tied
with dreams, and their craft and spells were stolen from
the genies in the bush country.
This is one of their stories.*

The Loom of Night

(Senegal)

Here is what was.

This is. This will be. It is a story.

There once were two weavers named Hammadi and Demba. When
Hammadi wove, the weave was tight and yet the cloth felt light to the
skin. His designs delighted the eye. Everyone wanted Hammadi's cloth.

Though Demba worked harder and longer than Hammadi, he was
slow and clumsy. No one desired his cloth. In all the land, there was not
a poorer weaver.

One day, his wife, Penda, held up his coarse creations. "No one
wants your cloth. They only want Hammadi's. Why don't you quit?
Become a farmer."

His wife's words hurt him, but Demba went on working at his loom. "Weaving is magic. I don't want to grow peanuts or anything else," he said. "These hands will never dig in the dirt."

"If you were a farmer, we might have something to eat," his wife replied.

Demba was tired of arguing. "There is a man in the next village who owes me a sheep. I'll go get it."

Penda looked at her husband in surprise. "It's the middle of the day. The genies are out now. Who knows what mischief they might work."

"You want food, but you won't let me go and get it," Demba said, exasperated.

Now, Penda was a wise woman and knew many odd bits of lore. "I see that you are set on leaving. Well, then, if you meet a genie, do not show fear. Genies admire bravery and despise cowardice."

Demba walked sadly out of the village, past the fields and into the bush country.

Demba's wife had voiced his own doubts. God, it is said, made all weavers equal; and yet everyone praised Hammadi's weaving, so he grew rich. At the same time, everyone despised Demba's, so he remained poor. He felt like a terrible failure.

Perhaps, he thought to himself, Penda is right. Perhaps I should become a farmer. But he loved to take thin strands of colored thread and weave them together into cloth. And he loved to take words and fashion them into poems and songs.

The bush country spread out endlessly before Demba, big and hot and hostile. Only small bushes and scrubs and spiny acacia trees grew from the dry soil. The bush country does not love people, for they clear away the trees and brush to plant their fields and build their villages.

The hot sun beat down on Demba's head, and the buzzing of insects filled his ears until he lost track of his thoughts. So he was grateful when he reached a river. Suddenly, in the hot, lifeless air, there was a twist of wind like a sigh. The dust whirled up as if someone had kicked it.

"Are you of the bush country or are you of the village?" a voice asked.

He turned and saw a woman kneeling upon the bank. Her face was hidden by her long hair which she was lowering into the water to wash.

"Of the village," he replied.

When she straightened up, he saw her hair reached past her waist and rippled like the surface of the river. Light sparkled from it like sunlight dancing on the water.

Demba said to himself, No one but a spirit of the bush country, a genie, could have such magical hair.

"And what have you come to steal from me?" she demanded harshly. Her hair crackled like lightning.

Frightened, the weaver opened his mouth to pray: May God protect us.

However, she raised a finger and pointed. "By Koumba Dieri, Koumbati Dieri, Fatimata Nyougourou, Salamata Kanka, Biri, Bafet, strike him speechless!"

Immediately, his words caught in his throat like the barbed bones of a fish, small and tight and sharp. His throat froze completely.

She smiled now. "Your kind has stolen everything from us—our lands, our secrets, our magic. What else can you want?"

Demba was so terrified that he nearly fell down. But he remembered his wife's warning and fought to appear calm. If he ran or fell to his knees and begged silently for his life, the genie would kill him.

Forcing himself to smile, he tried to tell her that he wanted nothing. Only little squawking sounds came from his throat. Still, he did not show he was afraid. Instead, he merely shook his head politely.

Then, kneeling beside the river, Demba put his hands into the water. Raising them, he drank—as if that was all he wanted. All the time, he knew the genie was watching him. Giving her another smile, he got to his feet and strolled away. He wanted to run, but he made himself amble along. Sweat covered his face, but he kept to a leisurely pace.

Once out of the genie's sight, however, Demba broke into a run. Though the heat was fierce, he ran. Though the dust choked his throat and coated his sweaty face, he ran. For his life, he ran.

When the farmers of his village saw Demba from their fields, they mistook him for a genie. His clothes were all tangled, and the dust covering his skin made him look strange.

Panting, he stumbled through the village to his house. When Penda saw him, she cried, "What happened to you?"

He struggled to tell her, but only tiny squawks came from his throat.

"You've met a genie," Penda concluded. "Didn't I warn you?" And she took him inside.

Penda sought help from the rest of their family, who all crowded into the couple's little house. They had all kinds of remedies for a stolen voice—from herbal medicines to charms and spells. They were still discussing what to do when night came. Exhausted, the weaver left them to argue and went to sleep.

In his dream, Demba heard a noise. When he went to his loom, he found the genie there. She stopped weaving and smiled. "I like people who can keep their heads. You're not like the rest of these chickens. The least little bit of magic upsets them."

So that night, she taught him what she knew of weaving. She showed him many practical things as well as magical spells. When Demba awoke the next morning, he found his voice had returned. "I feel wonderful," he said to his wife, and rushed to the shed behind their house.

As he sat before his loom of sticks, one of the genie's songs came to him. "Let me be strong as iron," he sang. "And let my fingers work quick and true."

Suddenly, Demba felt strong and quick. Then he began working as he sang another song:

This world with many wonders teems
Man and woman, young and old
From women all else streams
That's the truth: as good as gold
So let the threads come!

His hands had never been so nimble. The cloth seemed to fly from his loom. It was of such a fine weave that soon everyone in the village wanted his cloth, not Hammadi's.

The truth was that Hammadi already knew many magical spells himself, and some of them were evil. All this time, he had spoiled Demba's weaving with his sorcery. But the genie had taught Demba a song to protect him from such harmful enchantments. Hammadi's spells could not touch Demba now.

As the days went by and the cloth piled up, unwanted, in Hammadi's house, Hammadi became furious. "That fool learned a spell to protect himself. He must have met a spirit of the bush country. I'll go there and learn an even stronger spell."

So Hammadi traveled deep into the bush country until he came to a river. Suddenly, there was a twist of wind and a whirl of dust.

"Are you of the bush country or are you of the village?" a voice asked.

Hammadi turned and saw the genie sitting upon the riverbank. She was washing her long, shimmering hair. Hammadi thought the genie would be more likely to help him if she thought he was one of her kind. "Of the bush," he lied. "There is a person of the village who is evil. His name is Demba."

The genie narrowed her eyes suspiciously. "I know Demba. That does not sound like him."

Hammadi began to sweat with fear, for the genie reminded him of a lioness hunting her prey. "He casts spells upon me. He must be destroyed."

"A wish should come back to the wisher: good for good and bad for bad." As the genie leapt to her feet, her long hair cracked like a whip. Her nails grew long as claws and sharp as knives. They made hissing noises as she sliced at the air, exclaiming, "By Koumba Dieri, Koumbati Dieri, Fatimata Nyougourou, Salamata Kanka, Biri, Bafet, we have evil to end!"

Trembling, Hammadi looked up at the sky. Dark gray clouds swept toward them. He saw shapes and faces within the clouds, and they were terrible to behold. At the sight, Hammadi lost his nerve. He thought they had discovered his true motives. He opened his mouth to curse, but the genie pointed at him.

"By Koumba Dieri, Koumbati Dieri, Fatimata Nyougourou, Salamata Kanka, Biri, Bafet, strike him speechless!" she called.

Then only squawking noises came from his throat. Whirling around, Hammadi ran. For his life, he ran. He did not stop until he reached his house.

Exhausted, he went to sleep. In his dreams, the genie crept into the room. Behind her, like a mist, came Koumba Dieri, Koumbati Dieri, Fatimata Nyougourou, Salamata Kanka, Biri, and Bafet. And they were terrible to behold.

"So," she jeered, "you took our lands and our secrets and our magic. And now you would steal our honor and use us for your own twisted ends."

As they closed over him, Hammadi screamed and screamed, but no sounds came out. There was no one to help him.

No trace was ever found of Hammadi. Everyone thought he had become discouraged by Demba's weaving. They figured that Hammadi had gone off and set up his loom somewhere else.

Demba himself had little leisure to think about Hammadi. He was too busy making up for years of frustration. He had even less spare time to stroll into the bush country. When he did, he never went in the middle of the day. He had been lucky in his last encounter with a spirit of the bush country, but he might not be in his next.

DREAMS AND THE FUTURE

*Throughout the ages, people have believed that dreams can tell
us what lies ahead. The Assyrians and the Greeks had special
books to interpret dreams and predict the future.
Here is a Chinese folktale about a dream that does just that.*

The Buried Treasure

(China)

There was once a rich man who heard that there was no lock that could
not be picked. So he put his money into jars and buried them in secret
places. In fact, the whole town nicknamed him "Old Jarhead."

Now, Jarhead had two sons. The older son, Yuè Cang, already
managed the family's lands and properties. However, the younger son,
Yuè Shêng, cared neither for books nor for business. Old Jarhead
scolded and begged him to change, and each time the young man
promised to behave. However, he never remembered his promise.

Since Yuè Shêng was also a friendly fellow, he never turned a guest
away from his door. Often he had to provide meals for three or even four
guests a day. Everyone took advantage of him. As a result, his money
poured through his hands like water.

One day when Old Jarhead fell sick, he summoned his sons to his
bedside and told them the contents of his will. To the older son, he left
everything. His younger son, Yuè Shêng, would receive nothing.

Hurt, Yuè Shêng sighed. "Well, it isn't as if you didn't warn me."

Alarmed, Old Jarhead tried to sit up but could not. "I'm not
trying to punish you," he wheezed. "I have money set aside for you.

75

But if I gave it to you now, you'd spend it all. You'll get it when you've learned the value of hard work."

Despite his faults, Yuè Shêng was a good son. Bowing his head, he said, "Father, may the day of your death never come. May you live a thousand years."

However, Old Jarhead grew steadily worse and died shortly after that. Yuè Shêng wept until his eyes were purple, for he truly loved his father, though he had not listened to him. His older brother hardly shed a tear, for he had loved their father's wealth more than their father. When Yuè Shêng asked his brother about the burial, his brother replied, "I'm too busy. You handle it." So Yuè Shêng organized everything by himself.

Old Jarhead had been an important man in town. Yuè Shêng was determined that he should have a proper funeral. He ordered an elaborate coffin and then asked a priest to name a good date on which to bury his father.

On the appointed day, Yuè Shêng hired a band of musicians and scattered lots of glittering ghost money. Ghosts were too stupid to tell the shiny paper money from real money. They would be so busy trying to pick it up that they would leave Old Jarhead's ghost alone. At the graveside, Yuè Shêng set out a banquet for his father's spirit. At home, he put out yet another feast for the many mourners. He even let his father's tenant farmers have seats, though his older brother protested.

Everyone in town said the elaborate funeral was fitting for someone as important as Old Jarhead. Although Yuè Shêng had arranged everything, his older brother took all the credit.

Yet when the bills came due, the older brother passed them on to Yuè Shêng. "I would never have ordered anything so extravagant," Yuè Cang said. "This is much too wasteful. I refuse to pay."

The funeral had indeed been very expensive, so Yuè Shêng sold everything he owned to settle the debt. But when Yuè Shêng lost his house, he lost his friends. None of them would give him so much as a bowl of rice.

Naturally, Yuè Shêng went to his brother to borrow some money. He found Yuè Cang tearing down their father's old house. That upset Yuè Shêng very much.

"Why are you destroying all of our memories?" Yuè Shêng demanded.

"This old pile is riddled with termites," his older brother explained, "and I've found a much better place to build. I'm very busy, brother. What do you want?"

When Yuè Shêng asked for help, his brother sniffed. "Humph, I'm not going to feed every moocher in town. You're still much too wasteful." He gave Yuè Shêng only a few copper coins. "These will keep you from starving if you're careful. I have expenses of my own."

After this, Yuè Shêng went down to his brother's fields. Yuè Cang rented the fields to farmers who paid him with a share of their crops.

The tenants were surprised to see Yuè Shêng there.

"Please show me what to do," Yuè Shêng humbly begged them. "If I don't work, I'll starve."

One of the tenants, a fellow named Turnip Nose, grunted. "So your brother's so small-hearted that he turned his back on you. Well, your father was a nice gent. For his sake, I'll give you part of my share. But you'll have to work very hard."

"I'm not afraid to use my hands," Yuè Shêng said.

Each season, then, Turnip Nose told him what to do. In the spring, Yuè Shêng pulled the plow himself to turn up the soil. Next, he planted seed and weeded the rice plants and tended them. When the crops ripened, he harvested them and Turnip Nose gave him a small part of what they had grown. If Yuè Shêng was careful, it would be just enough rice to live on.

As year followed year, Yuè Shêng became lean and tough as wood. One day when he was washing up, he saw his reflection in the bucket and thought, If Father could see me, he would laugh. I certainly know all about hard work now.

That night, Yuè Shêng dreamed that he was walking on their old estate. He passed by two pine trees growing from the same trunk. Behind them was an old well that had been filled in. Next to it were the ruins of an old brick wall. Right at the corner, he dug beneath the foundation. And there in the dirt was a jar of gold.

As soon as Yuè Shêng awoke the next morning, he jumped up. Trembling, he went back to the site of his father's house. The walls had all been torn down, but the twin pine trees still grew. Beyond them, he found the well that his brother's men had filled in. Then he traced the remains of the wall until he came to the corner. With his hoe, Yuè Shêng began to dig.

When he reached the foundation, he heard a clink. Falling to his knees, he scrabbled in the dirt. Gradually, he uncovered a jar. With shaking fingers, he unsealed the lid. The jar was crammed with gleaming gold ingots.

Yuè Shêng lifted some of the heavy ingots into his hands. The sun shone from their sides. "This is the gold Father intended for me when I learned what work meant," he said aloud. Yet as he stared at them, he felt guilty. "But Father left the house to my older brother. By rights, the jar still belongs to him."

The honest man put back the gold ingots and covered the jar again. Then he went to his brother's house. However, the gatekeeper would not let him inside. "I'm sorry, young master, but your brother has ordered me not to let you in. He doesn't want to see you anymore. Please don't beg."

So Yuè Shêng asked for ink and paper to write a note. In it, he told his brother where the treasure was. Folding it up, he asked the gatekeeper to take it to his brother.

At first, Yuè Cang was just going to tear the note up without reading it. However, his wife scolded him, saying, "Your brother could be very sick. Imagine what people would say if he we let him die?"

Reluctantly, the older brother read the note. As soon as he finished, he jumped up and called for his servants. "What's wrong?" his wife asked.

The older brother rushed from the room, bellowing to his servants. Some brought his sedan chair; others snatched up shovels and hoes. Cursing and shouting, the older brother guided everyone to the ruins of the old house. Getting out of his sedan chair, he went to the spot described in the note and commanded his men to dig there.

When they had uncovered the jar, Yuè Cang told them to stand back. Then he knelt and lifted the lid. Immediately, he fell backward with a scream. When the curious servants peeked inside, they saw the jar was full of snakes. After the older brother had recovered himself, he straightened his robes and dusted himself off. "This is not a funny prank at all," he said sternly.

Getting back into his sedan chair, Yuè Cang ordered his servants to take him and the jar to his brother's hut. Yuè Shêng was sitting outside, eating a simple meal of rice with a few salted vegetables.

When Yuè Shêng saw the jar in a servant's arms, he set down his bowl and stood up. "What are you doing here?"

His brother glared from his sedan chair. "I'm returning your jar to you."

"But Father gave the house to you. The jar is yours," Yuè Shêng protested.

"No. It's all yours," his brother said, then gestured to his servants. As they all marched forward, one threw the jar at Yuè Shêng's feet. When it shattered, shining gold ingots spilled around his ankles.

"Where are the snakes?" the older brother asked, bewildered.

"There was only gold in the jar when I looked," Yuè Shêng explained.

Then Yuè Cang understood. "It's a sign from our father that this gold is destined only for you," he said. "This is the share he always meant to give you."

Although Yuè Shêng offered him the gold again, his brother refused to take even a share. So Yuè Shêng used the money to buy a house and fields of his own. But he was always careful with his money, for he knew his father was not likely to send him another dream.

A DREAM COMES TRUE

As fleeting as dreams may be and as disappointing as it can be to reach for them, we must go on trying. As this final tale from India shows, some dreams do come true despite the odds — if we can only keep our wits.

The Fool's Dream

(India)

In the empire of Rúm in India there was once a slave boy who bounced from one job to another in the palace. He never lasted long in any position but was sent from the garden to the stables, from the stables to the menagerie, and then to the carpentry shop. The boy always got bored quickly and made trouble somehow. Since he was so foolish, he was assigned to the jester, or Fool, who amused the emperor and lightened his day. However, even the jester became disgusted with him. "Not every fool can become a Fool," he said, and dismissed the boy.

Finally, the boy was ordered to wait upon the emperor and empress at night in their bedroom. It was the most-hated job in the palace. The emperor and empress were fussy sleepers. All through the night, one or the other asked for something.

"This is your last chance," he was warned. "If you make the emperor angry, he will hang you."

So when the emperor and empress climbed into bed, he would lie down on the floor at its foot. On hot evenings, the emperor would order the boy to fan him and the empress. Or he would have to fetch iced fruits in a golden bowl. There was always something to do.

81

As a result, the boy rarely slept. He constantly had to keep one ear open for an imperial command. If an indignant emperor had to wake him up, the boy knew he would be beaten.

In the daytime, the boy had to wait on them, as well. If he yawned, he would also be beaten. This rarely happened, though, because the emperor's daughter was often present. While she was about, the boy kept alert so he could steal looks at her.

At one banquet, she was particularly lovely. She's so lovely, he thought to himself. If only I were not a slave.

At that moment, the emperor held out his cup as he told a story to his empress. He did not look around. He did not even say, "Please." Dutifully, the boy filled the cup from his pitcher. Then he stepped back among the shadows.

But you *are* a slave, the boy scolded himself. So it will never be.

That night, because they had eaten and drunk so much, the emperor and empress went right to sleep. The boy listened attentively to their snores for a while, but eventually he fell asleep, too.

That night, he dreamed the most wonderful dream. He sat within a golden palace. Everything seemed so beautiful, so detailed, so real.

Then the empress herself walked up to him. In her hands, she held a bowl with iced fruits, which she offered him for his delight. Though she pressed him to take one, the boy was so astounded that he could only stare.

Behind him, he heard a soft whispering sound: ♪-♪-♪-♪. He turned and saw the princess and her ladies enter the room. Their silks made the snakelike sound.

One lady set a large silver bowl upon the marbled floor. Another lady poured warm water into it and a third scented it with fresh flowers. Then the princess herself knelt and began to soap his feet.

As he felt the warm scented water close about his ankles, the boy laughed in wonder. And as the princess began to wash his toes, he laughed all the louder.

Suddenly, the emperor's voice seemed to thunder through the dream palace. "What is the meaning of this?"

As an invisible hand started to shake him, the boy felt confused and surprised. Then with regret, he realized that none of this had been real after all. He had only been dreaming. He felt his happiness evaporate like mist.

Groggily, he opened his eyes, to see an angry emperor and empress standing over him. The emperor was holding the boy's shoulder tightly. The empress was scolding him, "Your laughter woke us up."

The boy was so sorry that it had been a dream, he forgot to apologize.

The emperor glared down at him. "Well, at least you ought to tell us what you were laughing at."

When he heard the emperor's question, the boy felt as if he had been plunged into a vat of ice. If he told the emperor the truth, the emperor would have him skinned alive for the insult to his family. A princess and an empress do not wash a slave's feet, even in a dream. It was the dream of a fool, he told himself. But I'd be an even bigger fool to tell it.

Frightened, the boy could only stammer, "It w-w-was nothing, Your Exaltedness."

The empress glowered. "It must have been something. You were braying like a donkey."

The emperor's face grew a bright red and the vein on his forehead stood out like a blue worm. "Do you know . . . how frustrating . . . it is . . . to hear someone laugh . . . and not . . . share the joke?"

Trembling, the boy nodded.

"Well," the emperor said through clenched teeth, "this is ten times worse."

The boy bowed. "I'm sorry, Your Exaltedness. If I could tell you, I would. But I mustn't."

By now, the uproar had brought a quarter of the palace into the large bedroom.

The emperor turned to his guards and roared, "Hang this wretch, and find me a slave without a sense of humor."

Now the commotion had also drawn the princess with her ladies. When she heard the sentence, the princess stepped forward in alarm, for she had noticed the slave boy, too.

"Father," she said, "I beg you to reconsider. Has this boy not served us loyally until now?"

"Well, yes," the emperor admitted reluctantly. The vein on his forehead stopped throbbing. His daughter could always coax him out of any foul mood.

The princess walked up to her father. "This boy's only crime is that he's forgotten his dream and is too ashamed to admit it. If you execute a good slave for such a small thing, how will the other slaves react?"

"I don't call waking us up a trifle," the emperor grumbled, but he could deny his daughter nothing. As she pleaded for the boy's life, his face gradually lost its redness and the vein in his forehead became normal. "Perhaps I was a bit hasty," he finally admitted.

"However," the empress argued, "you can't pardon him. If you do, others will keep secrets. Soon no one will tell us anything."

Caught between his daughter and his wife, the emperor compromised. "Put him in the dungeon and set a guard to watch him. When he tells us the dream, he can gain his freedom."

Helplessly, the princess watched the guards take the boy away. He was locked into a tiny cell in the dungeon and a guard was set over him as the emperor had commanded.

Often the boy lay down on the bench and tried to ignore the rats playing about on the floor. He wanted to sleep so he could relive his wonderful dream again. Though he never did, he comforted himself at least with one idea: The princess herself had saved his life.

Otherwise, life in the palace seemed to return to normal. The emperor and empress found a new slave—one with a sour disposition and a face to match. He had never been heard to laugh at anything. The emperor himself tested the slave with his best jokes, but the slave never changed his frown.

After a while, though, the slave began to wear on the emperor's nerves, for the slave's constant frown made the emperor feel as if he had done something wrong. More and more, he missed the cheerful slave boy, and so did the princess. But both were afraid to admit it to the empress.

One day, three mares arrived at the palace. Accompanying them was a letter from the king of Balkh. As the puzzled emperor and empress gazed down from their balcony at the horses, their vizier read the following out loud:

"To the so-called emperor of Rúm—

> One, two, three
> Who are they
> And what can they be?

Prove to me that you are worthy to be an emperor. If you are wise, you will tell how the mares are related to one another. If you cannot, I will come with my army and teach you a lesson in humility. I will take your palace from you, and I will set you in the stables to clean up after my mares."

Now the king of Balkh was not to be taken lightly, nor was his army. The emperor and all his court tried to solve the riddle. Were the mares sisters? Were they cousins? There were many possibilities, but the wrong answer would start a war.

So the emperor offered a reward to anyone in the empire who could come up with the correct answer to the riddle. Word eventually reached the dungeon, where the slave boy heard. He thought and thought until he had the answer. He asked his guard to tell the emperor.

By this time, the emperor was so desperate, he was willing to hear even the slave boy. When the slave boy was brought up from the dungeons, the first one he looked for was the princess. When she saw him, she smiled.

Encouraged, the slave boy asked the stablemaster to lead the three mares next to the palace. When they arrived, he ordered another servant to climb to the roof with a big jug of water and pour it on top of the mares.

As the whole palace watched from the windows, the water splashed upon the mares. One cantered fifteen yards nervously. The second trotted twenty yards, but the third galloped right around the palace and back again.

"Before I became your bedroom attendant, I worked in your stables. The third is the youngest," the slave boy explained. "See how energetic she is? And see how the second whinnies to the third? She must be her mother. And look at how the first mare whinnies first to one and then the other. She must be the grandmother."

The emperor was delighted, but the empress objected. "You can't trust the opinion of a slave boy—especially one given to funny dreams," she said.

"Slave or not," the princess argued, "I think he has come up with the right answer."

"Let it be written," the emperor commanded.

The slave boy added with a bow, "And may I suggest that you say the answer comes from the humblest of your slaves."

And so it was done. The letter was dispatched with the mares to the king of Balkh.

"If you are right," the emperor said to the slave boy, "you will have your reward."

The boy bowed. "The only reward I ask is to serve you, Your Exaltedness."

"You don't want your freedom?" the princess asked.

"Where would I go but here?" the slave boy said, looking at her.

Now the emperor was secretly glad to replace his new slave with his old, and so he gave in readily.

But none had time to enjoy themselves, for the king of Balkh sent back a new letter with three sticks.

To the self-styled emperor of Rúm—

One, two, three
Who are they
And what can they be?

I have been too easy on you if a slave could answer my first puzzle. So riddle me this: What is the relationship of the three sticks? Answer me correctly or I will come with my army and we will each take turns using these sticks to beat you.

Once more, the worried emperor summoned his court. Though they all examined the sticks, none could come up with the right answer. Finally, the princess suggested letting the slave boy look at them.

When the slave boy inspected them, he asked for a tub of water. After the kitchen slaves brought it, he ordered them to put the sticks into the tub. One stick sank immediately. One disappeared below the surface but stopped halfway. The third floated on top.

"What is the meaning of this?" the emperor asked his slave.

"I thought I recognized this wood. Before I became your stable boy and then your personal nighttime attendant, I swept the floors in the palace carpentry shop. This is an exotic tree from a faraway land. The first stick comes from the roots of that tree. The second comes from its trunk and the third from its upper branches."

"Let it be written," the emperor commanded.

"And," the boy added, "may I suggest this—that you say the response comes from the most foolish of your slaves."

That was the way the letter was written. Then the answer with the sticks was sent back to the king of Balkh.

This time, the king of Balkh sent only a letter.

To the self-deluded emperor of Rúm—

>One and two
>Who are you?
>And what can you do?

I still think you are more lucky than clever, so I challenge you to a contest of wits. I have a monkey who is the smartest creature in the world, for he knows the wisdom of the sages and the mysteries of the ancients. The wisest person in your empire could not best him in a debate. If your champion fails, I will kill him and then come with my army and make you the servant of my monkey.

When the court heard the penalty, no one would volunteer—neither nobles, nor scholars, nor priests—though all were learned people.

"What's to be done?" the emperor moaned.

"Let me go," the slave boy offered. "I have answered his riddles twice. Before I worked in your bedroom, your stables, and your carpentry shop, I tended your menagerie, so I know a bit about monkeys. If I die, it will be a small loss."

Even the empress had to admit, "You may have annoying dreams, but you are a brave fellow."

"Go with our prayers," the emperor said. "And may heaven inspire you in the contest."

The emperor would have outfitted the boy in all sorts of finery and given him an elephant to ride on. Further, he would have selected an escort from his own guard, but the slave boy asked only for an old donkey.

"But you are going as my champion," the emperor protested.

"Yes," the boy agreed. "But I am also the humblest and most foolish of your slaves."

The emperor reluctantly scrapped all of his plans. However, before the slave boy set out, he went down to the market and found a merchant who traded regularly in Balkh. "What fruit do we have here that they do not have in Balkh?"

The merchant pondered the question for a while. Then he said, "They don't have oranges."

So the boy bought a dozen oranges and put them into a bag. Then he left the next morning on his little mount and went to Balkh.

The king of Balkh was beside himself when he heard the emperor had sent only a slave on a donkey. And when he saw how humbly the slave boy was dressed, he became even angrier. "What kind of insult is this?"

The slave boy bowed. "It is beneath the dignity of my exalted master to send a citizen to debate an animal. So he sends the humblest and most foolish of his slaves."

"It will be a pleasure to remove your saucy head," the king of Balkh said, and he sent for his pet monkey.

So the monkey was brought in upon a velvet cushion carried by its own special slave. The creature scampered off the cushion and onto a golden chair just below his master's own throne.

The boy pretended to yawn. "May we dispense with silly arguments? I am bored with discussing the nature of the universe. We do it all the time in Rúm."

The monkey was intelligent enough to speak for himself. "O slave," he said, "how may we prove who is the superior in intellect?"

"By granting the other his heart's desire," the boy said. "You may even ask first."

The monkey twisted his head around to look inquiringly at his master, and the king of Balkh slammed his fist down upon his throne. "This fool is eager to die. So be it."

Then the monkey turned back to the slave boy. "Give me what I ask for or my master will slay you and all the people in your land."

The boy folded his arms. "And what is this strange, wonderful thing you lust for? Tell me, O silly beast."

The monkey leaned forward triumphantly. "Give me an orange."

"One? I will give you a dozen." Opening his bag, the boy took out an orange and tossed it into the air. With one hand, he caught it while his other hand slipped out another and threw it into the air, as well. In the wink of an eye, he was juggling twelve oranges before the astonished king and monkey. "Before I worked in the stables, carpentry shop, and menagerie, I was an apprentice Fool," he explained.

When the monkey saw the luscious fruit, he lost control and began to chatter just like any monkey. The king had to admit that the boy was wiser than his pet. "And," he added, "if you are the humblest and most foolish of the emperor's slaves, what are the rest of his people like? And how much wiser must their ruler be? Truly we should have your emperor for a friend. And so I will treat the humblest of his country as one of the noblest in mine."

He showered the boy with lavish gifts and gave him elephants and horses and soldiers and servants to go with them. So when the boy returned to Rúm, people thought it was the king of Balkh invading their land.

Frantically, the emperor squeezed into his armor, even though it was a hot day, and set out with his army.

However, the boy sent a magnificent messenger on an elephant to tell the emperor that it was merely the humblest and most foolish of his slaves returning home. He had brought his master many presents from the king of Balkh, who now wanted to be his friend.

The emperor shed his armor in ecstasy and greeted the slave boy as if he were his son. He wed the boy to his daughter, who was more than willing. Then he built a golden palace for them. Under its ornate dome, his wife washed his feet and his mother-in-law offered him iced fruits. And it was only then that he told his dream to the emperor and empress and why he had laughed.

"And now my dream has come true," he said, and laughed again.

AFTERWORD

A writer is a daydreamer by profession, so I have always been fascinated by dreams. Dreams are elusive creatures. The closer you look, the harder they are to see. When I once tried to keep a journal of my dreams, they became more dense, complex, and puzzling.

Dr. William C. Dement, the director of the Stanford Sleep Disorders Clinic and Research Center, has described the physical mechanism of dreams. The average person passes through several stages of light sleep into a deep sleep, back into a stage of light sleep, and finally into REM sleep. This is the stage characterized by rapid eye movements (or REMs). It is during this time that we dream. We then repeat the whole process over again. The cycle occurs five times during the average night—so in this way, we are rather like sleeping dolphins who rise and fall and then rise again through the layers of the sea.

This is what happens to us physically. What amazes me is the many ways we have tried to explain that experience. Throughout the ages and all around the world, people have tried to explain what happens when we dream. From the earliest times, people believed that their respective gods sometimes sent visions in the form of dreams. Tradition often placed the dream experience outside the dreamer's body.

One can leave the body, as in "The Rescue," or even enter another body, as in "The Fighting Cricket." In the realm of dreams, all normal barriers collapse. A person can also travel vast distances to find a true love, as in "Dream Girl."

For the dreamer, time itself collapses. A dreamer can cross the sea of time and see the future, as in "The Fool's Dream" or "The Buried Treasure." And as "South Branch" demonstrates, time literally has no meaning.

In a story like "The Loom of Night," dreams become the symbolic arena in which primitive, magical, creative forces like the genie can invade our ordinary waking world. Dreams are a raw, uncontrollable cousin to the creative act.

The inspiration of dreams can become preferable to waking life, as in "The Dream Tree." At the very least, in dreams, we may be able to recognize certain connections to the rest of the world that we ignore when awake—as the kind man finds out in the "The Helpful Badger."

However, as early as classical times, the Greeks had begun to place some of the influences internally. In the second century A.D., a professional interpreter of dreams, Artemidorus Daldianus, also explained that some parts of a dream came from within the dreamer and were triggered from memories of what had happened that day. In "Paying with Shadows," there is a clear distinction between events in the dream and events in waking life.

Psychiatrist Sigmund Freud later theorized that dreams were fashioned mostly from internal elements within the dreamer's mind. Events of the day—even a name spoken out loud—might create the platform from which a dream is launched. Our memories of the day can be broken up into bits and these fragments become attached to other bits of past memories. Moreover, the memory of every experience has an emotional charge like a battery and the fragments of memory carry their own amounts of charge. These pieces of memory and emotion then become connected until we get the dense, confusing parade of dream symbols. Since Freud, there have been many other psychological explanations for dreams.

External or internal, traditional or Freudian, dreams will continue to fascinate and inspire us. And so will tales about dreams. For we all know what it is like to reach for our dreams and grasp only shadows. Yet it is part of being human to go on reaching, for who knows? Like the fool, we may gain the wildest of dreams.

ACKNOWLEDGMENTS

The badger story comes from U. A. Casal's "The Goblin Fox and Badger and Other Witch Animals of Japan," volume 18 (1959), *Folklore Studies* (now *Asian Folklore Studies*). I wish to thank the editor, Professor Peter Knecht, for granting permission to retell it.

I also wish to thank Professor Roy M. Dilley for permission to retell one of the dream tales he published in "Dreams, Inspiration and Craftwork Among Tukolor Weavers" in *Dreaming, Religion and Society in Africa* (1992). I also want to thank his editor, Rosalind Shaw, and the publisher, E. J. Brill.

Works consulted for this collection are:

North Indian Notes and Queries (1895)

Somadeva Bhatta, *Kathasarit Sagara*

Xingu Villa Boas, *The Indians, Their Myths*, trans. Susanna Hertelend Rudge (1970, reprint 1973)

de Groot, *Religious Systems of China*, 6 volumes (1892–1910)

William C. Dement, *The Sleepwatchers* (1992)

Sigmund Freud, *The Interpretation of Dreams* (1913)

Douglas Gifford, *Warriors, Gods and Spirits from Central and South American Mythology* (1983)

Gérard Meyer, *Paroles du soir, Contes toucouleurs* (1988)

Plutarch, *Vitae Parallelae*, "Demetrios"

Pu Songling, *Liao zhai zhi yi*

ABOUT THE AUTHOR

The author of more than twenty books for children, *Laurence Yep* has received numerous awards, including the Newbery Honor and the *Boston Globe-Horn Book* Award. He has written two previous books for BridgeWater: *The Man Who Tricked a Ghost* and *The Junior Thunder Lord*. Mr. Yep lives in San Francisco, California, with his wife, Joanne Ryder.

ABOUT THE ILLUSTRATOR

Isadore Seltzer's wide range of illustrative talents can be found everywhere from graphics in major motion pictures to children's book illustrations. He wrote and illustrated *The House I Live In* and illustrated *The Man Who Tricked a Ghost*, by Laurence Yep. He lives in New York City with his wife, Joyce. They have two grown children.